CONCEALED

Under the Microscope of Disguise

—

Revealed by Faith

By: Saundra Kay Covington & Shekaunna T. McCauley
Published & Designed by: Lakisha Louissaint

This is a work of fiction based on true events designed to help those with or without traumatic experiences due to being bullied, mental, emotional, verbal, or physical abuse.

ISBN: 978-0-9992116-2-5
Library of Congress Control Number:2019914908
Printed in the United States of America

The Publisher, Designer, & Formatter is not responsible for ANY websites or anything outside of this manuscript.

Published, Designed, & Formatted by: Lakisha Louissaint

Acknowledgements:

I've been blessed with some amazing people in my life. First & foremost, without God, I wouldn't have had the courage or divine healing in & over my life. To my lovely mother Judy B. Covington, my god mother Ms. Eula Evans; my Pastor & First Lady, my amazing siblings, Lesia L. Johnson, Henry E. Covington Jr, Cynthia M. Covington; my closest friends Jennifer Mahand-Smith, Corcelia Hornsby-Lampley, Casandra Ware, Crystal James, Ken Valrie, Yalanda Brooks, Robin McKinney, Yolanda Daniels-Milton, & Marlon Snow your prayers, quotes, title suggestions, Godly counsel, & kind words of wisdom truly brought me through the darkest hours of my life and they will never be forgotten. To Andre & Kamythia March; Minister Charlie Jr., & Lady Pamela Ray Smith; as well as Mr. Patrick Hogan-Wise Boom & Jamilla Wise, thank you for being the A-TEAM of inspirational couples in my life. Mr. Jessie Youngblood thank you for introducing me to my dynamic publisher Lakisha Louissaint & being the best godfather that Shekaunna could ever have. Ms. Sheree Hardrick, thank you for giving my daughter & I the opportunity to speak to the youth Girls Supporting Girls. Finally, to the bravest daughter anyone could ever ask for Shekaunna T. McCauley who encouraged me which such powerful word, "Mom stop crying... you can do this. We're still here!" You rock!

Synopsis:

Her life was concealed to the world as she suffered mental, physical, and emotional trauma from someone that was to love her. His inability to receive the help he needed was finally revealed in that which only a microscope could see through eyes of faith through the invasion of privacy.

September 1992: How it All Began

Business was nothing new to me being that I was exposed to men ten to twelve hours a day five days a week for eight years. I was simply there for a pay check and benefits but, the new younger ladies were strictly there hoping they would serve an officer or gentlemen as their husbands. I was newly saved and I refused to allow some guy to use me as his trophy or worse, in which I witnessed too often. My job was simple, I would wait at the pickup door for bulk orders and check I.D.'s and invoice numbers with excellence. Later, my goal was to work my way up the corporate ladder as top buyer and travel from different branches all over the world. In doing so, the bonus would offer free education and training. You couldn't beat that. And so, it began in the month of September, in a small town in the south. The weather was hot, so I wore a teal seashell printed summer dress that hugged my thin waist, broad hips, and apple bottom. I wanted to look extra special since the Chief

1

Fireman and his small crew were visiting the company to view our new safety reflective designs for their fire fighters' uniforms. I had my back turned as I was putting my long natural curly hair up into a bun when I heard this deep voice, "You have a beautiful swan neck." Mind you, I didn't take kindly to being flirted with in a professional setting. As I turned around, I saw this Greek god standing at about 6"5' in height, well groomed, pecan tanned, beyond handsome brother standing so close I could smell his cologne. "Lord have mercy!" He extended his large callused, manicured hands with a smile, "Good afternoon ma'am." He paused, "I'm Mr. Rappt. I'm here for a Miss Kay to show me a potential firefighter order and you are?" I stood there like an idiot as his hand remained holding mine. When I'm nervous I bite the inside of my jaw to collect myself and that I was doing. I took a deep breath, "Please excuse me, I'm Kay Simpson. I wasn't expecting someone for another hour." He smiled, "Please call me Anthony. I'm a very punctual person and I was eager to see your new line. Our Chief is very ill, so I'll be in charge." His eyes never left mine the entire time he was holding my hand firmly with the other one placed on top. This was no ordinary man. He had all a woman could ask for. The height, intelligence, complexion, short curly hair, hazel eyes, deep voice, and a firm grip with a great job and a beautiful smile, but it appeared that he grinded his nubbed teeth and needed Lumineers. Three factors were confirmed within the next thirty minutes. As I escorted him to our warehouse, he said, "Jesus keep me near the cross, I've gotta stay saved to avoid hell. It's roasting back here!" (Check One). He began to fan with a naked ring finger (Check Two). Then, he bent over to pick up a heavy pile of jackets that had fallen from the conveyor table. Within seconds, he heard an openly gay worker make a cat call. With a firm stare, he replied, "No thanks man. I'm strictly heterosexual." (Check Three). I immediately asked for the young man's badge and reported him directly to the top for reprimand. He turned his attention back to me. "Wow, you don't play do you." With raised brows, I replied, "Not on the job! No pun intended. He knows better. He may lose his job this time. Sexual harassment is not tolerated on the workforce and you're comment about my neck was border line offensive." Embarrassed, he replied, "Please accept my sincere apology." It made me smile to know that he was impressed with my idea for the cooling installation. As we continued, I noticed the questionable reflective threads that were sewn into the jackets that were made overseas. This concerned me because we had no knowledge of what the glow in the dark substance was made from. Our company was noticeably cutting corners with our well reputation of quality not quantity motto. This reasoning was justified in a board meeting disguised as cheaper cost to save the company money, I guess my opinion during previous board meetings didn't matter because apparently, they didn't stop cutting corners. If I sold the deal, I would earn a hefty bonus and promotion and that would be a blessing. It was close to 5 o'clock and I'm sure he heard my stomach growling. That would explain why he offered to take me to dinner at 6:30 p.m. He asked, "Am I being too forward?" Needless to say, I declined the offer and gave him my business card, in case he needed it for additional information to discuss with his boss for a potential purchase. I had to go straight home to eat some natural and spiritual food, because I felt faint. The weekend passed with thoughts of this man even at church. Monday morning, my coworkers were talking about their dates and forthcoming events with their boyfriends and husbands. As they were talking one of my close coworkers noticed that I was unusually quiet and asked, "Aren't you excited about landing the recent $20,000.00 sale?" I nonchalantly replied, "Absolutely." She smiled, "Soooo, he wasn't that bad? Huh?" I was a little thrown off and replied with a smirk, "Excuse me?" With her brows lifted and a smile, she shot back, "I noticed how he captivated you, then ya'll exchanged business cards." I quickly thought...*Wow! You never know who's watching.* Taken back, I smiled, "Melissa, you know how professional I am. I don't fraternize with business partners. I don't want my past to rear its ugly head." Apologetically, she replied, "Oh yeah, I forgot." Confused as to her memory loss, I reacted, "You're blessed you don't have to remember." She looked at me, "Try to relax, you can handle yourself as always." I felt confident that this was my big break upon hearing my name announced over the intercom to the CEO's office. My pastor preached to us about being prepared for a blessing in an unusual way. He would say, "Be ready, even if you don't understand it." Instead of Mr. Gates being in his office, there was a panel of folks. I took a seat and within 12 minutes, I left numb. Inflation forced the company to down size in every way, unless I was willing to move overseas to Japan. I asked for a platinum departure that was in my union packet for events such as this. It was granted immediately. They knew if it were challenged, I would have filed a lawsuit. Notably, I assumed my recent large sale should've been worth $1,000,000 but I guess that didn't happen. I met Mr. Rappt standing at my office with my favorite flower's (Tulips) with a pink bow around the crystal vase. *How did he know?* As I walked towards him, he immediately knew I was upset. I smiled to hide the pain, "The flowers are lovely, but this isn't a good time." Coworkers were whispering and gathering for an explanation as other names were being called to be fired as well. I started packing a box with my belongings and he

5

kindly carried it to my car. I didn't even say good bye or explain my devastating news to the rest of my coworkers. "Anthony, I truly appreciate your help with my things and your bold persistence is flattering, but this is obviously not a good time to talk about my reasoning for not calling this weekend." He replied, "I can clearly see something is wrong. Please allow me to help you." I took a deep breath, "I was just fired based on inflation. My faith is truly being tested right now, but I have to continue to trust God." Tears flooded my eyes as I lay on his muscular chest. By the time I realized where I had planted my head, my knees got weak from his intoxicating manly scent as he wrapped his very strong arms around my waist. A breeze rescued my weakness allowing me an opportunity to apologize, "I'm sorry, it's the heat out here." He noticed that people were looking so he reach for my box, "Please let me take you away from here." I smiled, "No, thanks! I'll be fine. Besides, I really don't know you." He asked me if he could pray for me, so we walked under the shaded oak tree where we took our breaks. As we sat down at the picnic table, I was in shock. Not from being fired or the 98-degree temperature, but because this man asked to pray for me. I bowed my head with gratitude and listened as he prayed. "Father God, You said where there are two or three gathered in Your name, You shall be there. Calm my sister's storm and remind her that faith without works is dead and that You said You shall supply all of her needs. Restore all that is lost 100-fold and let her know that this was Your will and she will still be blessed. Peace be still in Jesus name Amen." With a heart filled with gratitude, I smiled, "Amen and thank you." He nodded, "I came here on business and to see you of course. Unfortunately, there is something wrong with our protective gear." Being that I wasn't in a good mood from being released from my job, the defects in their gear didn't matter to me. I really didn't care at that point. Before leaving, I looked up at him with a faint smile, "I'll call you later because I have to vacate this property, but thanks again." After I left, Anthony walked back in and approached my boss, "Is that why you let Miss Kay go?" Unfortunately, he wasn't at liberty to discuss such personal confidential status. In my defense, Mr. Rappt informed my previous boss that they lost a great worker such as myself and would later regret losing our business. He didn't stop there. He left him in shock as he walked to the door and turned back, "Your product is a health hazard and Mr. Gates, you will hear from our attorney." After arriving home and taking a long shower, I poured me a large glass of sweet red wine and shared the news with my family. Disgusted at their decision, I couldn't eat, so I sat up for a while since it was too early for bed. Finally, around 6:45 p.m., I mustard up enough nerve to call my handsome prayer warrior. He answered on the first ring.

"Hi there! Are you feeling better?" I confidently replied, "No, but I will be in time." He explained that he had to cancel the business deal due to allergic reactions from the reflective threads. Apparently, the gel was made of a toxic substance. He informed me that the CEO begged him to allow thirty days to fix the problem as they were in a financial crisis and needed to keep all potential buyers. As the conversation continued, he explained, "You left your Ms. Simpson marble name plaque behind." I scoffed, "It was intentional." He continued, "May I take you to dinner?" All I could do was smile, "I thought you'd never ask." All of a sudden, I was famished, so we met at a restaurant. I stepped out of the car in my skinny jeans and a satin floral printed shirt. He of course had changed from his business attire to a dark peach polo shirt and denim jeans. You'd think we planned it. As he pulled out my chair, he smiled, "Thank you for meeting me on this hectic Monday evening." He then held my hands very gently and blessed the food. I gave him an A+ for leaving his phone in his car. I considered that to be very respectful. As we ate, I shared with him the details of my unexpected, stressful day with his undivided attention. He informed me of his decision to cancel the order and possibly seek legal advice. He enjoyed his favorite, T-Bone steak and I ate my 8oz Ribeye with sides like a boss. I was thirty with no children and he was thirty-nine with two sons and two step daughters. He and I spoke with ease of our career choices and how we were both divorced. Not to mention, we were both believers and that was another A+ for me. When he mentioned my stern actions about the cat call situation at my former job, I took a sip of my drink and looked up, "I would have fired him on the spot, but I wasn't his supervisor. Besides, I had to go through the chain of command." Maintaining eye contact, I continued, "I separate my private life from my profession. You see, I survived being raped, sexually assaulted by a pastor in a local city, and sexual assaulted at another workplace. That in itself makes you become overly protective; besides I don't play about sexual harassment." I gathered myself, "The rapist committed suicide a month later and the guy that I worked for at the other company disappeared when I wrote him a resignation letter informing him that I would be reporting his unprofessional behavior and the fact that he patted my butt and rubbed me close to my breast. Oh, and the preacher settled out of court. Needless to say, I was under a gag order afterwards." He looked at me with empathy in his eyes, "I'm sorry. People like that don't deserve mercy, especially child molesters." He continued, "So, are you single?" I smiled, "Of course, besides, I wouldn't be here if I weren't. What about you?" He returned a smile, "Actually, I just got out of a relationship." He paused, "Now, I'm seeking closure." I was immediately turned off. I knew it was too good to be true. I took a sip of my drink as he explained, "I don't think it's fair to get into any type of relationship unless your past one is resolved. (Duh) I appreciated him for not playing me though, but I felt we shouldn't have exchanged contact information or even met for dinner since he hadn't moved forward from his previous relationship. I smiled, "So, I spoke with my family about losing my job, but I reassured them that I was in transition to a new direction in my life." I took another sip of my drink, "I plan on moving to Georgia to further my education and take advantage of the Peach Grant I was granted at my previous job." He smiled as I continued, "This supernatural blessing made me realize I was ready to earn a spot in the corporate world." Secretly, I wanted/needed someone to support and share my success with. I smiled, "So, Anthony my desire is to date for a mate." He cleared his throat, "I don't think I'm ready for that." In knowing that, the evening had to come to an end. I got my apple la mode to go and shook his hand farewell. He turned out to be a big disappointment.

"New Direction"

I've always loved children, so I was excited when I completed my Master's Degree with a double major in business and early childhood development. Besides, being a third-grade teacher would allow me to teach children since I couldn't birth them. You see, when I was seventeen, I was diagnosed with Sickle Cell Anemia and made the haunting decision to terminate my pregnancy because doctors warned me that a pregnancy could possibly cause my child to contract the same blood disease. Honestly, I felt this unwanted diagnosis was a curse because it was affecting so much of my life. After graduation, I left my siblings Leslie and Edward in Savannah to return to help take care of my mother who suffered from chronic depression with my middle sister Marie. There, I joined a local church and sang in the (AVOP) Anointed Voices of Praise Choir! I needed someone to hold my video camera and tambourine during our musical workshop and noticed a man who resembled my heart throb Anthony and asked, "Can you please keep an eye on my stuff while I freshen up in the ladies' room?" He politely replied, "Sure, what's your name?" I smiled, "Katie, but all of my friends call me Kay." He winked, "My pleasure, I'm Dennis." Since moving back from Savannah, I had developed an *It's All About Me Attitude,* so I winked back. After letting my curls down, I applied lip gloss, and a squirt of perfume on my wrist, behind my ear, and on my neck. I walked in slowly towards this man that all the haters weren't gutsy enough to approach and clearly flirted with him and smiled, "Thanks Dennis." He turned out to be an organist from another church that came to help our minister of music. It was obvious that I was instantly attracted to him and it was apparent that he was attracted to me. I was now thirty-four and desired to be married like yesterday. Besides, all of my friends and classmates were wives and or moms; some for over a decade. I was a bridesmaid for eight weddings, but never a bride of my own. I guess being physically fit with workouts and plenty of cardio wasn't working because I had yet to be proposed to. Regardless of being single, I remained active in the church, never smoked, but of course I drank a little red wine occasionally. Besides, I had matured and learned from my teen mistakes of promiscuity. I was lonely and sick of hearing my parents begging for a grandbaby and my clock was ticking, whether it be adoption or a miraculous birth. I made up my mind that I was going to make this man my husband!!!!! Shortly after the workshop I was invited to a restaurant by our minister of music and guess who was sitting at the head of the table? Mr. Delicious Dennis. This 6"3' light skinned brother had a smile that would brighten any room along with his four gold teeth that he wore outside of rehearsal. He told many jokes, but was very rude while texting and talking loud with food in his mouth. Sadly, he didn't pull out my chair as I expected nor did he offer to pay for my meal. During our conversation I discovered that it was his idea to use our mutual friend to invite me. So, I stayed and tolerated these two No No's. In other words, never allow desperation to cause you to lower your standards and receive treatment such as I did. Now back to the story. As we exchanged numbers, he kissed me on the cheek near my mouth and left me to pay the tip. I thought to myself, *He's a diamond in the rough and needed some polishing with abrasive sand paper* Lol. Needless to say, a year later, he moved in with me after we got married at an Elders house. I later became pregnant twice at thirty-five, but sadly they both resulted in miscarriages. Come to find out he dropped out of high school and had poor credit. My dad helped him get two full time jobs with benefits since he needed extra income to purchase a car. I tried to encourage him to enroll into school to sharpen his gifted musical skills being that he only played music by ear. In order for him to play with household gospel names and travel with lucrative pay, being able to read music notes was a requirement. My mindset was, (I) have my man and (I'll) change him really soon. What was I thinking? He had previously promised me a formal wedding and our own house; however, we wound up living with my parents until I discovered that I was expecting again. I couldn't bare living with my parents, not to mention I made a terrible mistake of selling my condo believing his lie about a house he never could afford. Although I was married and fully grown, we still had to abide by my parents' rules. I had developed a severe sinus infection and the antibiotic overrode my birth control pills. I knew she was a girl. Sadly, I later had to quit my teaching job due to it being a high-risk pregnancy. Dennis gained health risk weight, yet lost his motivation to support his family and sadly, his self-esteem drastically declined. It wasn't sexy to know that my husband's stomach was bigger than mine. His man breast were a complete turn off. I tried to encourage him to workout, eat healthy, and to take short walks with me, but that didn't work either. You would've thought Dennis had bad luck because he was hit in his head with a metal beam at work and had to have major surgery which cost him his job. Instead of him being patient and allowing his attorney to handle his case, he settled for $3,000.00. He could have sued them for millions and had his medical bills and legal fees paid in full. Instead we were living off of unemployment checks the first six months of our baby's life. I knew I had settled when he had the audacity to say, "When the baby is born, you can go back to work and I'll stay home to cook, clean, and be Mr. Mom to the baby, okay!" I thought to myself, *I just can't do it anymore. It's hard taking care of everything.* With a stern voice, I gave it to him, "You lazy bastard. You are worse than an infidel. If you don't work, you don't eat! I should've listened to your mother and sister when they warned me of your laziness and how your first wife took care of you. I'm NOT the one." I had taken out my braids and looked a mess. That wasn't good because at 33 weeks my water broke which sent me into early labor. My sister took me to another close by hospital because my amniotic fluid was soaking everything and my husband was at church practicing with the other musicians claiming that he didn't hear his phone ringing. I prayed aloud, "The devil is a liar and his mama's name is sin! I'm not losing this baby too. Pretty or not here she comes." The entire staff laughed. I had an emergency Caesarean section to a tiny princess weighing 4lbs 4oz and she was 17 inches long. It was a miracle. I didn't have one sickle cell crisis or miscarriage during my 7th months of pregnancy. So, I gladly embraced those painful staples. The only true pain I had was the spinal tap. Sadly, I didn't even get to hold my little princess because she was immediately rushed to another hospital. All I had to see was eighteen staples and a love line. The doctor informed me that I had a complicated delivery specifying that my daughter was never born, but delivered. Needless to say, I felt some kind of way. Later, the doctor's informed me that I had postpartum depression due to not being able to hear or hold my little princess after her birth. Once we were reunited, I felt a disconnect; however, I felt that doctor and nurses' comments after my birth had something to do with the depression since they made me feel less than a woman and mother. As far as my husband was concerned, the Bible clearly say's in Proverbs 18:22...He that finds a wife, finds a good thing. The words came back to me loud and clear. "I'm going to make him my husband!" I was convicted and totally out of order. I truly loved Dennis, but I was desperate for a family (A Baby) and with knowing that he wasn't prepared to support us on every level was a bad move on my part. Especially since we were singing and playing songs in the choir that we weren't living by. I couldn't take it anymore, so, I repented and asked God to forgive me. I didn't want my choices of willful sinning to continue to affect our lives or our daughter whom we named Shannon Glory McSnell. After twenty-one days in the premature ward, I was able to bring her home in a used carriage. I even had to borrow a used breast pump machine so that I could feed her. We were borrowing from Peter to pay Paul (Late). We were living off of unemployment, Food Stamps, WIC, and any other governmental assistance available in which was fine with him, but it irked me that he wanted to take the easy way out. We stopped praying together and our arguments became frequent. My dad lost total respect for Dennis when he found out how he was treating me and that he failed to take care of us financially because he wanted me to be the bread winner of the house. He was no longer Dennis to my dad, he was now referred to as boy, but as for my mother, she was happy to have another grandbaby and my siblings frequently reminded me that I could do better than him. Instead of riding his bike to work, he would steal my car. Quite frankly, I felt that he could have ridden his bike instead. My sister Marie never forgot the day she saw me walking two blocks to get to work while I was three months pregnant because he didn't have the money to get his car fixed and no insurance. So, he asked me to walk to work instead. He had to work much earlier than I did and justified it by saying, "You're used to taking walks. Besides, you're much closer to work than I am." I shook my head, "I'm not being mean, but you have put on at least fifty pounds since my first trimester. You really need the exercise." Just say he stole my keys again. SMH!!! I left for work thirty minutes early and asked God to send me an angel and that He did. She promised not to tell my parents or black belt brother, but whatever she said to him that evening, he came back with my keys and an apology and I never had to walk to work again. He weighed 320lbs by the time Shannon came home. In addition to that, Dennis started drinking and smoking and I was fed up. I refused to continue to take care of a grown abled body man and he didn't get a pass from me to check out on his family. Although he was hurt on his job and had a neck brace on for several weeks, he could do light duty work until he was stronger. Not to mention, he no longer came home and he stopped playing the organ. One morning, I woke up at 3 a.m. to check on Shannon and found him moaning and groaning while masturbating to porn of young girls still in their puberty stage on our rent to own computer. We didn't own a microwave, so I quietly took the pot of boiling hot water that I used to warm my baby's milk since my nipples were too cracked to breastfeed and threw it on him while he was reaching his climax. As he screamed, I busted him in the head with the pot, "You will never touch me or Shannon again. You damn pervert." This would explain why he wanted to bathe and change her diapers and never wanted anyone to babysit her. I stared at him with tears rolling down my face, "I won't compete with this foolishness." Sadly, he refused help in any way. He wouldn't exercise, stop smoking, or drinking. He even refused to return to work. The day Shannon turned nine months, I swallowed my pride and did what I had to do for survival. I moved out in the very same apartment complex with the help of governmental assistance. With concern, the rental manager looked at me, "I'm so glad you left that loser. He asked me to sleep with him on the side as well as my neighbor who has five kids by four different daddies." I continued to hear similar accusations from friends and church members. I wish someone would have informed me of my husbands' infidelity when it started because it would have given me the opportunity to watch, pray, or leave him. It hurt that no one was woman enough to tell me. No woman wants to be the last to know that their man is cheating or doing other stupid stuff. That's embarrassing. What I really wanted to do was tell all of them to go to the place where the devil lays. I began questioning why I didn't discern that spirit amongst others. Oh yeah, I probably couldn't hear God's voice because I was in my own will, doing my own thing, while out of His will for my life. Since our divorce was uncontested, I was divorced in sixty days. SMH, we didn't last two years. As granny used to say, "Some people are meant to be in your life for a lesson, a blessing, or a lifetime." I love seasoned folk! They're so full of wisdom. She warned me about Dennis, but I didn't listen. She said, "His hands are too pretty for a man. He doesn't like to work; he just wants to be a pretty Boy!" And that was no lie. It was now me, myself, Shannon, and I.

Me, Myself, Shannon & I

I was thirty-nine with a four-year-old baby girl and single. I changed my name back to Simpson but I let Shannon keep her father's last name. My mom and granny didn't keep their married names either. They believed it was best to go back to their maiden name. I remember when I was younger, how my mother ran away with my siblings and I from Tennessee to Alabama in the middle of the night to get away from her husband; my deceased biological father who cheated on her and beat her as an alcoholic. I always thought I'd see a huge letter (S) on her chest. She struggled to support us, but she kept us and herself safe and alive by her heroic act. My mama would say, "Never stay attached to anything that will hurt you." I asked mama did granny have sickle cell since she and my daddy had the sickle cell trait? She nodded, "The old wives use to say it's a family curse in people of color because the blood is too close." She told me that when grannies parents died when she was thirteen, she became pregnant with me at age fourteen by her uncle, who raped her. She told me that my daddy is my great uncle. I wished grandmama would tell her story. She said people her age take stuff like that to their graves. Followed by, "I'm glad I'm here and you too shugga puttin. Just praise God that that plump butterbean baby don't have it. Kay, be sure to stay in church." I did as she asked by staying active in several auxiliaries like the choir, singles ministry, youth ministry, Sunday school teacher, announcer, food bank/open closet helps, and the women's ministry as well. I even read many self-help books that were beneficial to my life that encouraged growth along with attending multiple women retreats. I meditated on God's word in Psalms, Proverbs, and Acts. I even fasted for thirty days, which was a huge accomplishment for me being that I have Sickle Cell Anemia.

I got my finances in order and I worked in retail management for a season. Meanwhile, little Miss Shannon thrived from breastmilk. Although I was hospitalized from a crisis and had to get help raising her, she became my motivation to be a great example before her eyes. I made sure that she and I dressed alike, played, prayed, sang, and read at bedtime without fail. She went from plump to an inquisitive little girl who didn't want for anything, but an earthly father. My dad was her only active father. Although she was only six, I think she handled his death from prostate cancer very well. I spent the remaining $50k of my departure money from my former job on my mother's medical bills since she'd suffered a nervous break-down from my father's passing. During a tragic incident years ago, my daughter who was now seven, bless her little heart, donated her favorite doll, hair ribbons, and clothing to a little girl she'd met at a youth retreat who was also affected by the tragedy that struck where we lived. But nonetheless, our small town came together as one and rebuilt our city back stronger than ever before. We were so glad to be a part of our sister's cities restoration. As adults, we naturally worry about our children; however, this tragedy confirmed how resilient the children were and how they were able to cope and bounce back after such a tragedy. Shannon and her cousin Marias birthdays were five days apart, so, I decided to give her a

$3,000 ninth birthday party. She had water slides, jumpers, magic shows, party favors, food, a six-horse carousel, and the icing on the cake was a little tea cup Chihuahua, she named "Pepper." Although her dad was invited, he didn't show up, only her uncle who she mistaken for her dad and his wife Dee. Dennis missed out on so many first of his oh so beautiful daughter's life that looked just like him and it was certainly his lost. Although he was made to pay child support, cutting her off was so selfish and I truly don't see how he slept or sleeps at night. I'm no longer angry nor do I cry for my daughter not having her father anymore. I simply continue to pray that God would change his heart. Maybe someday when she's old enough, I'll share all that her father did and didn't do as my mother did with us. Meanwhile, I never spoke any negative comments about him around her. He had visitation rights but only with a supervised liaison present in which he declined the judges offer and refused to have someone to watch him push his daughter on a swing at the park or get ice cream. He would much rather pay child support of only $100.00 a month because his work history was so poor so he chose to keep his distance. To me, he was a piss poor excuse of a father, but Shannon was the best blessing out of that relationship I could ever have. As time went on, I had to be very careful who I chose to date because Shannon would become attached and call whomever I was dating dad! That's enough to understandably scare any man away; therefore, I prayed to be a good judge of character because all she wanted was a daddy and quite honestly the single life sucked and wasn't for me. I loved my girlfriends but I was sick of hanging out with them all of the time and hugging my pillow at night. Mama once said, "Be patient, wait on God, and pray for a discerning spirit before you date again." I do love seasoned people, but that was easy for her to say after being married for over thirty years. I felt sad for her because being a widow was very similar to a divorced woman since they both suffer a death whether slow or sudden.

Mr. Rappt

When Shannon was a toddler, I quit my job in retail management and returned to work as a teacher, but I began losing my zeal for it. One day my Ride or Die Chic Candy took Shannon and her daughter Marie to Panama City Beach, FL for the weekend. I on the other hand decided to spoil myself with a new haircut, a day at the spa, and a movie. Popcorn and children are the noisiest sounds at a theater. Nowadays, children are totally disrespectful. I witnessed a child kicking and screaming at his parents, swearing at them, and throwing his popcorn. He had to be at least twelve years old. Before treating myself to dinner after the movies,

I swore I saw Anthony Rappt. As I was driving off, I almost rear ended someone while staring into that massive crowd trying to wave at this fine man. I smiled, "Lord, it should be a crime to be that fine." Needless to say, I had to repent for lusting after this man I once craved. During dinner I wondered why he was alone at the theater or wasn't he? Had he resolved or rekindled his past relationship or was he single like I was? Having a business degree came with big advantages like being able to work in an administration department. So, a month later, during a job fair on a local military base, a position was open that offered hands on training, a 401K, their vacation offers were second to none, and I would be able to negotiate my pay. To live in this area of Alabama where it's economically reasonable to live, no high crime, great school systems, and so close to Ga and Fl., I stepped out on faith and put in my application because I was confident that I could land the job. I felt that since it was at the end of the school year, the transition would be smooth. In waiting for an answer, I saw Anthony's oldest son Nicholas whom I learned worked in the school system as a janitor. I remembered his handsome face, but never made the connection because of his first name nametag. He saw me from the floral department and came over to speak. He smiled, "Hi Ms. Kate I told my dad you loved tulips because you always had them on your desk and I had to sweep up the

24

petals all the time." I smirked, "Oh dear Nick I'm sorry." He shook his head, "It's okay. My dad asks about you all the time. After that lady Ms. Bethany broke his heart, you're all he thinks about. Will you make it up to me and call him? That could make up for having to sweep up all of those flowers over the years?" With a smile on my face, I replied, "Sure. You drive a hard bargain!" We both laughed. "Do you have his business card from the Fire Station?" He shook his head, "No ma'am. He had a bad accident with somebody dying in a fire and it messed him up in the head, so he retired early. He's been working as a lead engineer for nine or ten years now in the machinist department. I thought to myself, *Wow! We may be working for and at the same company soon. But why would his son share such personal information with me. Shannon knows I would whip her behind if she disclosed any of our business without my approval. A bad reflection of parenting if you asked me. Thank goodness it wasn't truly private information.* He later wrote down his dad's contact information and extended it to me, "Here are both of his numbers. Do you want his direct office number too?" I shook my head, "No thank you. You've been quite informative." He continued, "I made supervisor and you won't be seeing me much because I'll have my own office. Just say that I'll be shoveling paper's instead of sweeping them." I thought quietly to myself, *you won't be seeing me either if I land this career opportunity*. He replied confidently, "Those are some bad asses at that school, huh?" He quickly apologized as I stared at him in shock. Clearly, he realized he overstepped his boundaries. That evening I mustard up enough courage and video called Anthony. He answered on the first ring. "Hi, thank you for calling! I've been expecting you to call me. How are you? How have you been? Oh! I saw you pass by at the theater. My son say's you look great." I thought loudly, *shut your pie-hole man and get a frigging grip!* He was clearly embarrassed when I didn't respond and immediately apologized. Finally, I responded, "Hi and take a deep breath. It was exciting to see you as well as your son." He asked, "So, did you like the movie?" Excited that he took notice of my presence at the theater, I quickly replied, "Yes, but do you recall at our first and final dinner, I don't bite my tongue." He nodded as I continued, "So, I have a few questions to ask." He replied, "Shoot!" I took a deep breath and gave it a go. "Are you married, divorced, single, in between a relationship, widowed or dating absolutely anyone?" Taken back, he deeply inhaled and exhaled, "Whoa! You take a deep breath!" I continued, "Touche...Please answer the question truthfully." He looked me straight in the eyes, "I'm single by choice." I thought to myself, *He's so arrogant*. He must've noticed my eyebrow lift because he cleared his throat, "I really meant that I haven't found anyone to settle down with and I finally closed the chapter to my previous relationship." Although it's a metaphor, I didn't like the expression settle down with. It made me feel like a person who accepts less than their worth. He sat down and adjusted his phone so that I could see him on the screen, "Yes ma'am I do recall, you do shoot from the hip. I see you didn't waste any time moving to Georgia." I thought to myself and smirked, *Whew! He has my undivided attention.* "Well I'm too old to play games and I've come to know my self-worth. I don't play second best to anyone." I thought to myself, *now who sounds arrogant?* He smiled, "I noticed that peach floral shirt you wore to the restaurant." I gasped with amazement, "Well, I've gotten somewhat too thick to wear that shirt anymore." Then he bravely replied, "I love a woman with a little meat on her bones." Again, I thought to myself, *I bet he heard that in a movie,* but I didn't bust him out on that quote. We shared various topics that flowed from a variety of subjects including the prayer he prayed for me under the shaded tree when I got fired. Not only did he have a great memory, he also listened without interruption. What a breath of fresh air. There's something about the art of communication. He made me feel so comfortable that I quickly became transparent about my personal life. Although I was intrigued for more, he was considerate enough to end our informative conversation at a respectful time. Just say, I went to bed like a school girl reminiscing.

Courtship

Anthony loved, horror movies, wrestling, and, all other sports unlike myself. Oddly, on our first date he took me and my daughter to department stores to trick or treat. She didn't dress up, but I thought it was a nice gesture that he wanted to meet Shannon and include her on our first date, but the cold weather made my joints ache. So, he opened the door and got out with Shannon holding her gloved hands, carefully observing their surroundings while never leaving my sight. He was a complete gentleman as he opened our doors, carried Shannon's candy bag, and closely examined her individually wrapped candy before consumption. I smiled, "Her dentist said she may need braces soon, so she can only pick two of her favorite pieces of candy." He agreed, "You can never be too careful these days. They're so many evil people in this world, especially when it comes to our children huh?" His statement made me wonder had something bad happened to him as a child or one of his children. I nodded, "Yes sir, you said a mouth full. Shannon knows all about 'stranger danger'." She seemed to like him, especially since he had learned her favorite color and flavored ice cream, not to mention, they shared the same birthday. I wasn't really worried because Shannon and I had a secret code just in case she was ever in trouble. She would say my favorite color is red (Meaning Help) or she would use anything red to alert me as a cry for help. In our lengthy conversation, he asked questions about me as well as Shannon. Both of our eyes popped and mouths opened. when he asked, "Shannon, did you enjoy the pony rides at your ninth birthday party?" Puzzled, Shannon replied, "Uh huh. Yes sir." With squinted eyes, I chimed in, "How do you know?" He smiled, "My best friend Gil mentioned that your mom had ordered it for her birthday and I asked him to allow me to pay as a birthday gift!" Shocked, I thought to myself, *that explains why Mr. Gil said the horse carousel was paid in full.* My heart smiled, "Thanks so much Anthony." His masculine scent became intoxicating as we hugged three seconds too long. I used Shannon's napkin to fan with as she smiled, "Thank you so much Mr. Anthony." I smiled and watched as she thanked him, then it hit me. *If we ever start a relationship, I won't ever allow her to call him uncle.* The thought of that reminded me of a guy I dated briefly who insisted on Shannon calling him uncle. It makes things creepy and awkward if the couple decides to marry later. I quickly snapped back to reality as he drove us home in his Lexis Coupe. Although it isn't ideal to put someone in the backseat of a Coupe, Shannon's small frame fit perfectly. He winked, "I plan on trading this car in when the dynamics of my life change." I smiled as he got out and opened the door to my three-bedroom townhouse effortlessly holding Shannon in his arms as she slept peacefully. "Kay, what about a nightcap?" I smiled as we walked in, "I'll be right back. I'm gonna tuck my little princess in, then I'll get your night cap." Anthony waited patiently for me to bring him coffee, made exactly like he and I both liked it; two splashes of French vanilla creamer, no sugar. It wasn't customary for me to have a man in my house after the first date; however, my joints ached in my right leg and arm from a previous sickle cell crisis. Besides, since Shannon fell asleep, it would've made it more painful for me to carry her. It was only 9:15 p.m. when he departed. As he left, he placed his hand on my shoulder, "Thank you for being a breath of fresh tulips. Make sure you get some rest." Before walking out of the door, he turned back and prayed for me. Once again, this man was sensitive enough to have a coffee night cap, depart at a sensible time, discern my discomfort, and gently lay hands on my shoulder to pray for me, "By Jesus stripes you are healed." He closed the night with a soft kiss on my forehead and smiled, "I look forward to our next chapter, if you care to write the story. Good night." Veterans day, Thanksgiving, and Christmas, then New Years were memorable chapters we wrote together in a serious relationship. We compromised our faith/salvation by sleeping together in which he blamed on the alcohol. I thought it was a cop-out because we willfully allowed our flesh to be gratified period. One mother who saw me the following Sunday smiled, "I missed you at watch night service honey." All I could do was hold my head down in shame after repenting at the altar. She continued, "Once you wake that monster up, there's no rocking it back to sleep." She was right. I began day dreaming of how I got to this place. Later that evening, Anthony and I got dressed in our black and silver outfits, ate dinner, went dancing, and kissed passionately to our favorite song. He wasn't much of a drinker, but red wine was my thing and he took full advantage of that as he constantly poured me extra glasses to drink. Not to mention, I felt guilty about not going to watch night service, something his church wasn't accustomed to. Besides, Shannon was with my sister Marie and her twin grand babies. We went to his place for a night cap and this time it wasn't coffee. Our work schedules never clashed. We had coffee dates, visited Shannon's school plays, shopped, cooked together, and much more. I had a new job as a buyer and a new man that started to become like my family. I thought to myself, *but if he liked it, why hadn't he put a ring on it? Pump your breaks girl*. It's only been four and a half months. I didn't want to rush ahead and find myself married and divorced twice, but there were some things I needed to know about this seemingly potential Mr. Right. As time passed, we began to get closer and I wanted a no holds bar so to speak pow wow with this man, so we decided to meet at a local park. It was necessary that we drove separately just in case a deal breaker occurred that way I could just say deuces and be on my way. As we sat and talked, transparency flowed like a waterfall. "Anthony, there's more to me than you know." I poured out my heart about the abortion, my detailed illness, my dreams, and desires. I boldly asked, "So, have you ever been arrested, incarcerated, had any illnesses, HIV, AIDS, or HPV?" Just say we purchased an STD home test kits. Thank God all of his results were negative. Let me tell you, Mark 14:38 told me that the spirit is willing, but the flesh is weak. To be real, that was no excuse. As we candidly revealed ourselves, he asked, "Have you ever had any homosexual experiences or threesomes?" Without an attitude I honestly replied, "No." I couldn't be mad because I asked him very private yet necessary questions in which he satisfied me by answering. He continued to share how he suffered from anxiety and depression. With regret in his eyes, he explained, "Because of my former career, I couldn't save a mobile home from burning. Remembering the sounds and screams from the little girl who hid in her closet remains branded in my mind and still often haunts me. That's why I don't care for open fires, candles, or mobile homes for that matter. And that doesn't help with me being a twenty-year Vet in the Marine Corp. The conversation didn't feel like an interrogation, just honest and factual conversation as we continued to get to know one another. He ended it perfectly by handing me beautiful multicolored tulips followed by, "Would you be my lady?" I smiled, "Sure!!! I thought you'd never ask." He then invited me to his church the following Sunday for the first time. Perhaps no mother there will ask me did I attend watchnight service at my church.

Psalm 150

Let's just say his faith and mine became a deal breaker five times after my first visit to his church. Their beliefs and doctrines were the total opposite of Psalm 150:3-6 which speaks of singing with a joyful noise, tambourines and cymbals. As for them, everything was acapella. For example, when I willfully sinned with Anthony, I asked God for forgiveness at home and at the altar; however, when they sinned, they stood before the congregation to confess their sins, ask for forgiveness, and then prayer. After an extensive conversation, I looked at my husband and said, "Anthony, we're jeopardizing our faith by having sex before marriage. I just want to be a good example for my daughter and not cut off my blessings. Besides, God is not pleased. It's better for us to marry than to burn." Each time he justified it with, "Kay, God knows our hearts," as if God was supposed to wink at our sins. And before I knew it, I experienced the episode of his anger. As I continued to visit his church, my spirit became vexed because there were no instruments in the church, the women were only allowed to teach, sing, cook, serve, and were never allowed to preach. Not to mention, they believed in communion every Sunday. In my opinion, my personal experience and their frequent attempts to convert me to their way of thinking and their beliefs affected my spiritual growth. I just didn't feel the presence of God there; therefore, causing me to feel that my attending their services were null and void. One day I walked over to Anthony and said, "Hey, can you take Shannon to minister in praise dance?" He raised his voice, "Dancing in church aint of God and she ain't no minister." I shot back, "Oh, but fornicating is?" (Crickets) I ended the relationship and took her myself. Before I knew it, he was begging us to come back so that we could pray for wisdom, knowledge, and understanding of God's Holy word. Once I returned, he reached for my hand, "Kay, our love for each other is strong enough to conquer all confusion." I shook my head, "Anthony, I get it, but God is not about confusion. He's all about order. Enough is enough. I'm done compromising both physically and spiritually. It's just not worth it anymore." I knew he suffered from PTSD (Post Traumatic Stress Disorder) as he had shared with me from his military and firefighting background, but this outburst and loud tone was downright scary. I immediately prayed for his deliverance of that angry spirit. Of course, we made up after he apologized and promised to go to anger management or change the strength of the anxiety medication he was on because I no longer wanted to fight over our being unequally yoked. As time passed and I tried to support him as he did me, but my question to him was, "So Anthony, what makes you think that your church is gonna be the only ones to make it into heaven?" I reached for my Bible and pointed to Revelation 7:9 a great multitude which no one could number. He smiled and nodded, "That's us that the Bible is talking about." I decided I wasn't gonna get into an argument over that with him, especially since I clearly can't add to or take away from the word; however, it did concern me that we were unequally yoked, no matter how much we loved each other, but what's love got to do with it. I remembered how my grandmother used to say, "Chile you don't argue with the truth." So, I took her advice.

The Proposal

Before I knew it, we were approaching another Thanksgiving, Christmas, and New Year together. We had experienced family reunions, movies, the beach, funerals, birthdays, promotions, vacations and many more outings together. We were a family. Well, at least we were acting like one. One day when we were getting ready to attend a close friend and co-workers wedding, I looked through the mirror at Anthony, "Ant is this the right type of jewelry for this dress?" He smiled as I continued, "Can you help me with my necklace because my arm is aching?" I paused, "Anthony can you zip me up please?" I realized there was no response. As I turned around, he was kneeling down on one knee sweating, an apparent anxiety attack. I panicked, "Oh Lord! What's happening?" Shannon ran in the room. "Momma, what's wrong with Mr. Anthony? He has a pretty box behind his back." In panic, I ran towards him, "Ant are you ok?" He smiled, "I would be if you'll marry me! We love each other and I want to make you my wife and Shannon my daughter." He looked pitiful when I delayed. As he continued, it seemed as though he had read my thoughts. "We can get marital counseling before marriage to work out our differences in our faith and I can take some financial classes to learn to manage our money together. Please baby, I have faith in our love. If it'll make you feel better, you can remain at your church and I'll remain at mine with the understanding that we support each other at least once a month. I'm trying to be reasonable and make this work. I don't want to lose you. I want and need you in my life Tink!" Just say I got the nick name from a night gown he purchased me for Valentine's Day. My dad raised us to believe if you have any reservations about anything, pray, think twice, and speak once. While this man was yet on one knee, Shannon smiled from ear to ear, "Mom are you gonna answer him?" I reflected on my first marriage, it was all about what I wanted, I rushed. It wasn't God's will. I willed myself to believe our love, (Mine and Ants) would conquer our faith issues. Then I heard myself say it! "YES!!" Shannon responded with excitement, "Yippee, I can finally call him DADDY!" I guess he liked it so much, he finally put a ring on it!!!!

The Wedding Plans

We dated for two years and finally decided to become a real legal family within a year of planning. He and I never experienced a formal wedding and since we were blessed to have the income to do so, we wanted to go all out. We started by making sure that we got all of our physical exams and dental work out of the way. Anthony had to get a few cavities extracted and had to wear a thick rubber retainer to keep him from grinding his teeth due to anxiety and eating a lot of hard candy. My oldest sister Leslie asked to be my wedding coordinator, my middle sister Marie was named my bridesmaid, my ride or die chic Candy accepted my proposal to be my Matron of Honor, I asked my sister in law Val and Anthony's two step daughter's Anita and Ashley to be my bride maids, Shannon would be my junior bride maid, and my great niece Melody would be my flower girl. At the age of 42, I was finally walking down a long aisle in a soft pink designer wedding gown with a six-foot veil and a huge crystal crown. I must say my hired personal trainer paid off, because I fit my dress like a glove. I know because the whispers and haters confirmed it. Leslie really made my fairy tale wedding come true with a beautiful cotton candy pink and light grey color theme. My pastor smiled, "Before I pronounce you man and wife, remember what your fourteen-day marital counseling taught you. Pray for wisdom, understanding of God's word, and don't allow your beliefs to be a wall to divide you." Anthony leaned me back and tickled my tonsils as Mrs. Anthony Devile' Rappt. After we jumped the traditional broom I screamed, "I'ze married ni!!!" Our reception was at the company's ball room where we had two hundred and fifty guests. The chef prepared the best succulent seafood shipped from Alaska, our all white cake was three feet tall with four different flavors which included lime, red velvet, vanilla, and chocolate layers. Fresh flowers were placed from top to bottom in every shade of pink, white, accented with silver. We hired a household name photographer and a photo booth that was activated with a completed well wish card, and a D.J., announcer who catered to all genre's and ages. I felt like a queen. All of the ladies ooooed and awwwwed about my four-karat diamond baguette platinum ring. Anthony gifted me a custom-made reception mermaid form fitting gown, as an exquisite bridal gift. Mama and grandma didn't care for it though. They said it didn't leave much to the imagination because of my cleavage and low-cut back. *Lord, what would they have said if they saw my teddies given to me at my bridal shower!* During the wedding, all of my senses were stimulated seemingly all at once; the smells, the sounds, the site of everything. I think you get the point. During the ceremony he looked at Shannon, "This is for you, a father's promise. I vow to love, protect, provide, and treasure you as your dad." Everyone cried. It didn't stop there. To see the smile on Shannon's face during her first daddy and daughter dance was absolutely delightful. After the dance he placed her opal birthstone around her neck with two small diamonds on each side to represent their shared October birthdays. My heart spoke within, *He's going to make an excellent father*. He repeatedly complimented her, "Shannon, you're absolutely beautiful. You're gonna grow up to be as fine as your mother. I couldn't see it because in my eyes she would always be my little princess. But Wait! Let's take a pause and back up. Now that I look back, that was sign #1. (Remember There Are Always Signs) Now back to my story. We had our first dance as husband and wife to our favorite song along with well wish toasts from family, friends, and co-workers. During the reception, my ride or die chic and only brother made subliminal threats to my now husband, "If she's ever hurt or unhappy..." I'm sure he got the point. We took hundreds of photos, tossed the wedding bouquet, and garter belt, then at the stroke of midnight, we secretly departed in our stretch limousine to the ATL airport to Bora Bora of France in the Pacific Ocean. Ant made sure a nurse was present with knowing that latitude could possibly trigger a sickle cell crisis, so he carefully planned not to have our honeymoons climate too hot or too cold. Another trigger, he took the time to educate himself about. We discussed taking all necessary precautions to avoid pregnancy due to our age and my medical condition. So, the shot was necessary because if I hadn't been on the Depo-Provera injections, I would have possibly become pregnant. Just say, I was very fertile. Our honeymoon was delightful in knowing that we finally did everything right in God's sight. All of the fun caused me to become dehydrated which was and is a No No. I walked away only for a moment only to return to see him dancing with another woman. (Sign #2) Although this offended me, some

40

battles aren't worth fighting, so I didn't even mention it. The next night I had an acute chest syndrome crisis and needed medical attention immediately for I.V, oxygen, and morphine drip. I asked Anthony to lay hands on my chest and pray over me. His reply baffled me, "I don't have time for that foolishness, let's get the doctor's hands on you in the ER." I thought I would die, not only from the pain, but from what I heard. I rested the entire day from fatigue, sore chest, and sore joints. As he left at noon to go horseback riding, I remained in bed budgeting our wedding and honey moon expenses. I was taken back that we had spent $6,000.00 over our budget. I had to dip into my 401K, which was a huge No No, but he assured me that we would rebuild it. Thank God we didn't have to put any money down on our humble five bed room, five-acre new home we had purchased with both our names on the deed. By 6:00 p.m. I was famished and called for room service. Surprisingly, an older Island woman came to my room and offered to prepare me a detoxifier meal to help build my blood and oxygenate my body. I sat up in the bed very weak and listened very carefully to this well-educated woman with no lines in her face, and wavy silvery white hair in a tight bun. The halter sun dress she wore accented with a small pair of opal earrings exposed her toned bronzed shoulders and arms. The phrase Black Don't Crack certainly, applies to this mother.) In her beautiful

Jamaican accent, she spoke sternly, "Chile stop taken all those controlled substances before it controls you and keep your bowels stopped up." I welcomed her to have a seat on the foot of my bed. She sat down and smiled, "I had to see you personally after hearing of your illness and the order of food you requested. No! My dear.... You need kale, spinach, bok choy, turnip greens mixed with beets with a pinch of Cayenne Pepper in a soup form. They're high in folic acid. This aids in improving your appetite, cell production, and red blood cell formation, along with plenty of no iced water for hydration." With a sense of peace within, I smiled, "Yes ma'am, you're so right. I just want some coconut milk and a burger." With a concern in her eyes she replied, "What you want and what you need are two different animals my dear." I inquisitively asked, "Are you a nurse? She smiled, "No my child, I am the Islands physician. I am Dr. Sees, not S-e-a-s. Now eat and drink 8 ounces of water before midnight for complete restoration. Don't have no more babies and give these earrings to your baby girl!" My heart skipped a beat! "How did you know?" She smiled once more, "Chile, I told you me name is Dr. Sees. It's not only because of your blood disease you shouldn't bare anymore children. In time you will know why. Once you lay eyes on her put these earrings in her ear, they're her birthstone-yes!" I nodded, "Yes ma'am." She continued, "Many believe these precious stones are formed by rain, which seeps down into the crevasses in the rock. Once the water evaporates, the silica that is left behind dries out and hardens into opal. It also symbolizes hope and good fortune for those who are pure in heart." Before departing she asked permission to pray for me. You see, earlier that day I told God that I needed my mom to pray for me and He sent this mother. I closed my eyes and bowed my head while weeping uncontrollably as she prayed. "Dear God Almighty we know we are sinners and we ask for Your forgiveness. We know and accept that Jesus Christ is Your Son. We know that He died for our sins and that You raised Him to life. We trust Him as our Savior and follow Him as Lord. Guide our lives and help us to do Your will. I pray this in the name of Jesus. Amen." She stood up from my bed, "Your soup is being prepared and will arrive in ten minutes." Before I could even ask, she turned to me with the sweetest voice, "I know you're saved and if you believe prayer without waivered faith, you'll receive your healing and much more my child. That prayer was simply a reintroduction to you rededicating your life to a Father who loves you." She then firmly said something that sent chills down my spine. From her Jamaican accent to Spanish, she spoke, "Manteerla Cerca," which is translated "Keep her close." I knew what she said through drilling Shannon's Spanish vocabulary words with her in elementary, but when she said, "I can smell yo mon, he be comin." I couldn't figure out what she meant. I figured it was his cologne I purchased for one of his wedding gifts. When Anthony came in, he smelled like cigars and liquor. He looked at the disgusted look on my face, "Chill out woman. You know I don't smoke. I was at the sports bar watching wrestling with some guys I just met, until it became a boob bar. You know that you're all I need. How you feeling?" I sat up, "My soup is on the way. Oh, and I had the most interesting guest. Her name is Dr. Sees and she told me about my diet and even prayed for me." He scoffed, "Oh! That ole hag I just ran into? That dickweed don't need come here again. She smelled funny." Shaking my head, I replied, "Please don't use that ugly word anymore. It may mean stupid, but it sounds much worse. She meant well." Nastily he replied, "Whatever makes your monkey jump!" While he was in the shower, a soft knock and room service sounded from the outside door. I covered up, "Please come in." It was a very beautiful young girl ordained with opal jewelry from head to toe. She looked angelic. Speaking softly, she placed my soup on my night stand, "Me grand mama say's to eat and drink eight ounces of wa ta before midnight and you shall recover. Good night ma'am. Be well." I smiled, "Thank you sweetie, here's a tip baby." She returned a smile, "No mum, rest easy." Anthony had enough sense and compassion to allow me to rest completely. I woke up refreshed, renewed, rejuvenated, and restored, just as Dr. Sees said. He decided to send her multi colored tropical flowers to represent the opal hues. He apologized for his poor choice of words and was glad I felt better. We spent the next ten days in marital bliss walking on the island, enjoying the best foods, wines, and festives while relaxing with dual massages. Not to mention, our last evening there was absolutely amazing because of the fireworks exploding over the crystal-clear water. I will definitely continue to eat that soup Dr. Sees made for me and make a mental note of all the wise words she told me.

The Life of Mrs. Rappt

Our wedding party and church families learned of my illness while away through my daily text with Shannon and an email I sent my sister's for prayer and decided to be a blessing by setting up our new home to relieve me of any stress that could potentially lead to a sickle cell crisis; except for our sacred master bedrooms décor. I couldn't wait to hold and kiss my princess and shower her with all the souvenir's I purchased for her, my family, friends and of course the gifts for our entire bridal party for helping us jump over that broom. Shannon greeted us with a Welcome Home banner (A Very Sweet Gesture) and I gave her the biggest hug and kiss. Anthony walked up to Shannon and smiled followed by a fist bump, "Hey Boy!" (That was Offensive) I looked at her, "He won't say it again. Just ignore him. He's jet lagged." Anthony reached down, picked me up, and carried me over the threshold for the second time, only this time it was inside our new home. I could feel the peace of God as we entered. Just say, I requested for a minister to pray, anoint, and bless our home before we returned and that she did. When Anthony finally put me down, I was overjoyed as to how perfectly put together everything was; as instructed. All of our gifts flooded our living room and our television screen read play me. It was a recording of our wedding and reception. After everyone left, Shannon and I sat and chatted for a while since we had never been apart and had so much to catch up on. Not to mention, she absolutely loved her earrings from Dr. Sees. Anthony shedded a tear as we all hugged and smiled, "You two have given me my heart's desire, a complete family." It's nice to see a man express his sensitive feelings. I just pray it remains that way.

Vows Put to the Test

My doctor had recently taken me off my contraceptives due to health reasons. Some weeks later I noticed a weight gain of twenty pounds which struck concerns as to possibly being pregnant, but thank God I wasn't. It was later obvious that Anthony wanted my tubes tied since he refused to get a vasectomy. He was so freaked out about an erectile dysfunction due to something being wrongfully cut. Needless to say, we both were alarmed to discover a month after a marriage that my pap smear was abnormal and my period was heavier than normal. A few weeks later, Anthony accompanied me to see my OBGYN. The doctor pulled up his chair, "We need to schedule you for a DNC (Dilation and Curettage) to stop the heavy bleeding. If the DNC failed to do its job, then getting a tubal ligation; my fallopian tubes tide would be next. Until then, it would be wise to use other contraceptives to avoid pregnancy," in which we both hated. Sadly, the DNC was unsuccessful causing me to faint and bump my head on the concrete floor while at work. Anthony later met the EMT's and I in the ER. Angry and replying with sarcasm as usual he said, "If you wanted attention and to take off work, all you had to do was say so." In disbelief I replied to the nerve of him, "Really Ant. I'm bleeding to death." He knew I was pissed and attempted to erase his inconsiderate remark, "Come on, I was only trying to get your mind off of this madness." I took a deep breath, "Please call my scared coworkers and my mom to let them know I'm stable and that the doctors won't have to admit me." Selfish with no consideration, he replied, "I'm your family. That's all who needs to know." Being careful not to become frustrated and trigger another crisis, I calmly replied, "Honey please understand. I don't want them worrying." Still lacking empathy, he looked away, "No one needs that much attention. I'll let you call who you want to know your business." Smh! (Shaking My Head). Shortly thereafter, I had to have my tubes tide. Needless to say, the next eight weeks were very stressful because I had to miss work, recover, rely on Anthony to cook, clean, and help Shannon with homework. If only he had a simple snip, his down time would have been within twenty-four hours, marital bliss within three days, and no time off of work. I could have been prescribed birth control pills to shrink the eight-cyst found on my ovaries to prevent getting my tubes tied after the DNC procedure. Oh well! Here we go.... I had to have a blood transfusion and was given a compatible blood type which they matched, but I almost died. Just say my recovery time was ten weeks. During that time, I remembered the soup Dr. Sees made and had my big mama (Granny) to duplicate a huge portion of it to regain my strength. Although Anthony was great in the kitchen and held it down with house chores, he still made Shannon attend his church. This decision compromised her choir practices, praise dance rehearsal, and time helping with the food bank ministry. Neither was she accustomed to attending church whereas the rocks cry out for you! (No Music, No Praise). She privately shared some disturbing things which occurred at his church in which I later planned to address. It bothered me that she was uncomfortable telling him of her discomfort and concerns of missing what she was used to at our church. To prepare Shannon, I discussed possible adjustments before I was married, but I didn't realize this would be one. It was gonna be a challenge for us to adjust to another person in our lives, (A Man, a Husband, a Dad). After all, it had been she and I for ten and a half years. Patience look out, here we come.

Sugar to S@%T (16, 12, 38)

Anthony was standing in the doorway with his feet and hand crossed with an evil smile on his face when I arrived home from 3rd shift. I loathed the working hours from 10 p.m. to 6a.m., but it was the only available shift allotted to me with the seniority I held. So, I toughed it out and sacrificed my night sleep so that I could be active and a part of my princess life. I walked in and gave him our morning customary kiss, "Why the silly grin on your face?" He laughed, "You're no longer the other woman in this house." I was confused, "Come again?" As I handed him my belongings he smirked,

"You know what I'm saying?" Reality is, I didn't know what he was saying. He continued, "Shannon needed a plug since she's now on the rag!" Another asinine statement. I ran beside him, "Oh Lord! My baby." He shouted, "No, another woman, I told you!" I was furious, "Wipe that silly grin off of your face so I can tend to her properly." Shannon had gotten her period at the tender age of twelve. Thank God I had given her "the talk" when she was 9 after her elaborate birthday party. Let's say she had a scare. She thought that she was pregnant from holding a boy's hand at school. At least that's what her classmates told her. That day I took her to the library to read books, pamphlets, and watch videos on anatomy. She then learned about me terminating my pregnancy when I was seventeen. She didn't respond in a gross manner, but the mature attitude, "Momma, it is what it is. I washed really good, took some medicine for my cramps, and I put on a pad just like you showed me. When I asked daddy to make me some hot tea, all he did was poke fun and kept saying you're a woman now huh!" That was insensitive. So, I informed him that poking fun of her during such a delicate time in her life was mean and thoughtless and I decided to deal with him later. I kept Shannon home with me instead of sending her to school and cared for her all day with maybe three hours of sleep. Later that day, I chewed Anthony out, "Look, your thoughtless comments about Shannon's period was unnecessary, I don't like that you continue to make her miss service at our church, and I'm tired of you hurting our feelings when we're sick. If you don't have anything nice to say, please don't say anything at all." Even in all of that, when he wanted dinner and bed time, I felt obligated to give in no matter how tired I was because if I didn't, he would preach about my body not being my own. He went as far as to post the scripture of 1 Corinthians 7:5 on my mirror after the doctor released me back to work. He would manipulate scripture by reminding me how we are not to deprive one another of sex. Sooooo, I would fix a quick bowl of soup, a salad, a sandwich meal, and give him what he wanted. With that biblical fact being said, he made sure that family was to be my first ministry. If I did anything contrary to his manipulation of The Word, there was hell to pay. He had to work from 5 p.m., until 1 a.m., and that seemed to be the only time of peace that Shannon and I had. When he arrived home, he refused to let our previous argument about Shannon go. My brows furrowed, "As a matter of fact, the same way that tea would've soothed Shannon's cramps, I thought make up sex would have settled it. Why are we still talking about this?" Per his lack of empathy, he replied, "Yeah, I know, I helped raised girls and even showed one of them where to put the tampon!" OMG (Oh My God)! He stopped in his tracks and stuttered, "On

You Tube of course." I didn't believe a word he said. Still hot, I replied, "There's no need for Shannon to be educated about her period, her hygiene products, adolescence, sex or anything of a sort. She's good!" About 9 p.m. when my night sitter had arrived to be with Shannon til 6:30 a.m., I got a call from Anthony saying we should go on a much-needed trip. (Crickets) I cleared what I really wanted to say from my throat, "Thanks for the great news. We'll do a monthly spread sheet of finances and see the more suitable way to spend it." We had borrowed money from my brother and sister to help cover our reception expenses since we went over budget and we really needed to pay more on our mortgage and principals on our new home. I was a stickler on paying bills in a timely manner as well as paying more than what's required on credit cards. It was important for me to show Shannon the benefits and responsibility of being a good steward of the 90% we had left over and the importance of keeping a high credit score. When I returned home, Anthony had cooked a wonderful breakfast with a fresh cut rose from our garden with a fun trip list with our ninety-day combined $2,500.00 bonus for no injuries from work. I was like, "WOW! Great minds think alike. I made a list too." We ate our breakfast, paid my night sitter, and sent Shannon off to school. I took a long shower while praying to God for the correct words to approach this money matter. I realized we were newlyweds getting to know one another better and compromising would keep the peace, but this man told me he would give me his pay check to manage our income since he trusted my financing abilities and would only have a $100.00 for pocket money bi-weekly. That didn't happen. Not to mention, he gave his best friend Gil in which he knew I didn't care for a major credit card to hold from spending and not me, his wife. So, I respectfully listened to his immature thought process without interruption. I then smiled and dared not to turn over the list of how we should spend our money to him. I smiled, "Can we split our bonus three ways? $1,500 to my sister and brother, $500 to the house, and $500 to Panama City Beach, FL for a weekend. We could use my nephew's military housing discount since he's active and we can use your retired military discounts for gas and food. Our activities can be crabbing, fishing, and hanging out on the beach as a family playing volley ball." He yelled, "Hell Naw! Your sister is a doctor. She ain't hurting for no money. She said we could pay it back whenever. We signed a thirty-year contract on this house. They don't care about principals, just the mortgage payment. I don't won't no food stamp budget trip to FL. You've changed. You ain't fun no more. Tell you what, I'll keep my bonus and do what I want with it." He did just that! Shannon and I didn't see or hear from him for "16" hours! This was supposedly said by a

God-fearing man who wears at least seven hats at his church, works hard, cooks, and calls us his Queens and Princess's... had now become mean spirited, selfish, and unable to manage money to save his life. He returned home Sunday morning about 2 a.m., "Sorry, me and Gil went to a basketball game." I was shocked, "You agreed for me to manage the money. Don't ever worry us like that again." He smirked, "My bad." Not to mention, he snored and stopped breathing eighteen times that night. I couldn't rest from having to roll him over and tapping him on the shoulder to wake him up. So, I slept in the guest bed room since he refused to wear his sleep apnea machine.

12 Days

We shared an office with opposite desk computers and filing cabinets. Whenever his ink would run low, he would use mine since he would print his church announcements every week and that was fine with me. He saw my bonus spread sheet of how I chose to spend my money. Based on his loud tone, he had an issue with it. Shannon immediately dismissed herself by slamming her bedroom door. He stared at me, "I found out how you used your bonus money." Confused, I replied, "We couldn't come to an agreement, so you spent your money how you wanted just as I did. The paper is self-explanatory: $500.00 each to my sister and brother, $250 on the principal, $100 savings, $100 car maintenance, and $50 on Shannon's praise dance uniforms. What's the problem?" He yelled, "Your sister could have waited!" I shot back, "It's the principal and our word. Our wedding expenses didn't have to wait, did they?" When he stood up, he intentionally pushed his office chair into my right knee cap hard enough to break the skin. I fell to the floor crying and screamed, "Look at what you've done to me!" Shannon rushed in to help me up, "Ma did dad hit you in the leg?" I wouldn't lie to her. So, I answered, Yes and without an apology." I reached for her hand, "Shannon wait, don't say anything to him or anyone else. I will handle it." Just say, my knee remained swollen for three days. Not to mention, he didn't speak to me for twelve days because he said I disobeyed him. WE'RE ... IN ... TROUBLE!!!!

38 Days

Anthony had been taking extra overtime, which was something he normally would have passed up especially since he loved to sleep in from going to bed at around 4 or 6 in the morning; however, our cable had been disconnected and our car insurance had lapsed, so the extra hours were necessary. He explained that he had to send money to place his mother in a facility because her insurance wouldn't cover it. Not to mention, he had to pay on her late taxes for some property she owned. I always kept the house immaculate and dinner prepared as I truly enjoyed. Side Note: I have six 1st place trophies and plaques to prove it from our Soul Food cook off at church. Anyways, that evening at around 6 o'clock, Shannon was in the dining room completing her school project when the doorbell rang. I thought it was my sister dropping off a check to take my mother shopping since we had become her conservator and guardianships over her assets, due to her chronic illness. To my surprise it was the Sheriff! My knees buckled and my heart began to race as I nervously asked, "Officer, may I help you? Is there something wrong?" He asked, "May I please speak to Mr. Anthony Rappt?" Confused, I replied, "He's not here. Is he hurt?" I felt panicked so I took a deep breath, "Please sir, what's this about?" I paused, "He's at work, but I'm his wife." He kindly handed me the papers, "Please give these to him immediately. He's been served." With wide eyes I replied, "Oh really! He's being sued?" He tilted his hat, "Have a good evening ma'am." Concerned, Shannon asked, "Mama what does you've been served mean?" Still confused, I walked past her, "Baby, this is grown folk's business. No need to worry. I'm getting to the bottom of this right now." I always made it my business to not disturb him at work, but this conversation couldn't wait. He answered his office phone as head supervisor, "What's up Tink?" I didn't have time for the small talk, so, without hesitation I laid it out on the line, "You just got served by the county Sheriff. What in the hell is going on?" He nonchalantly replied, "Oh, I got the notification in the mail yesterday." I thought to myself, *no wonder he broke my daily routine to rush and get the mail.* He continued, "I tried to call them to keep them from coming to the house or my job." At this point, I was over it, "You're more concerned about telling them and not me your wife? So, you're keeping secrets now? You're committing financial adultery on me too! Who's suing you and for how much?" He replied, "A major credit card company for $5,800 and court cost." Lord have mercy, I had to take another deep breath, "Really! I can't even deal with this, Shannon's calling me." Shortly after checking on her homework, quizzing her on English, and preparing dinner, I told her to clean the kitchen once more. Being that Shannon was diagnosed with ADHD and easily overstimulated, I had to constantly redirect her. In doing so, it kept her focus off of the dysfunction in the marriage that could possibly trigger an anxiety attack for her since she couldn't handle arguing. Still baffled by Anthony being sued, my level of becoming an independent CIA and FBI went to a whole new level especially since I had access to everything. I turned on the printer and made copies of every document from A to Z in his filing cabinet. Bank statements, bills, insurance policies, tax returns, social security cards, VA forms, retirement, recent purchases, and medical documents. I thought to myself, *why did he recently change his cell phone access code. I'll get that too.* I smell a rat! So, I made copies of everything in his filing cabinet until I ran out of ink, then I placed the documents in my trunk until I was able to thoroughly investigate what else he had been keeping from me. I didn't finish until 9:30 p.m. Just say that I arrived to work late. When he came home, I blatantly asked Anthony to explain why he failed to tell me about the letter, the Sheriff, and his decision not to tell me about one debt situation. He looked away, "I didn't want to worry you." I took a deep breath, "We aren't supposed to keep each other in the dark about anything." Deflecting, he replied, "Remember when you committed financial infidelity on me before?" I scoffed, "No, explain." Taken back by my response, he reacted, "I guess you forgot the damage you caused when you paid your sister that bonus money even when I told you not to." I dismissed his dumb comment and thought to myself, *Is he on drugs?* I calmed myself before answering, "What are we going to do to fix this? Is there anything else I need to know?" Sarcastically he followed up with a reply, "No, I'm good!" I thought to myself once more, *we sure aren't. Now I'm married to a bald-faced liar!* All of the copies I made revealed that our mortgage was late, he had taken out four loans, and our cell phones that he had changed in his name as a family plan were about to be disconnected. I went to the trunk and handed him the documents, "Anthony, explain this." He scanned over them and threw them towards my chest, but my aching arm blocked them. In disbelief, I looked at him, "I'm living with a liar, a verbal, and physical abuser, a man who keeps secrets, can't manage money, and God only knows what else. "After that Sheriff came, I had to know what else you were keeping from me. I'm your wife Anthony Rappt!!!" His brows met, "If you snoop in my business again you won't be my wife. Believe me, that's not a threat, it's a promise." The stress caused a full-blown sickle cell crisis. I could literally feel my blood cells sickling and clustering in my veins. I needed oxygen, I.V for hydration, and a controlled substance to eliminate the severe pain in my joints and lower back. I felt like I was being stabbed over and over with an ice pick. It was a life-threatening situation, in which Anthony was well educated about. You see, I made sure I educated my family, friends, neighbors, co-workers, and church family about how to help save my life. The longer I had to wait, put me in danger of more organ and bone damage. He took his sweet little time getting ready to take me to the hospital as he called in to his job. I didn't understand that because he was covered with medical leave of absence. He could've done that on the way there. Not to mention, he could've alerted the hospital that I was on my way. So, I called my sister Marie to pick me up with a whisper left in me. Thank God she wasn't that far away at a mutual friend's house. She heard the whisper in my voice and knew the severity of getting me medical attention. On her way to get me, she had Candy to pick Shannon up from school and she called my job. While Anthony was in his office on the phone, she scooped me up and left a note on the counter "Gone to ER with my sister." Needless to say, he got there an hour later after I was stabilized. Marie, Candy, my mother, and Shannon were yelling in the hallway in disbelief when he got there. He looked at my sister with sarcasm all over his face, "What are you mad about? Ya'll seemed to take care of my whole family, so what's the rush?" Livid, Candy looked him up and down, "You're a complete jerk!" Then Marie looked at him, "Really! We wouldn't have had to take care of your family if you would've stepped up to do it. This is my sister's life you're playing with. If she calls me, know that I'm coming to see about her period." As Shannon was crying, mama leaned over to console her. As mama gave Anthony a dirty look, I just prayed and screamed within with my eyes shut tight. Before the doctor released me, he spoke to me with great concern, "Whatever has you this stressed, you'd better get rid of it quickly or die from it." Taken back, Anthony looked at the doctor, "So what are you implying

Doc?" Not knowing that my husband was the stress he was implying of, he replied, "Sir, I didn't call anyone by name. My grandfather had a saying: If you throw a rock in a pack of dogs, the one that yelps got hurt. This metaphor means your response makes you look guilty." (Crickets) The doctor continued, "I would advise you to avoid three major triggers. As he named the triggers, he tapped his fingers, "Number one, stress. Number two, dehydration. And Number three, a lack of rest." Before he walked out, he turned back with a concerned smile, "Take care of yourself, okay." After being released, Candy made sure I was tucked in, had my meds, liquids, heating pads, and miracle soup (by Dr. Sees) at my bed side, as well as my portable oxygen machine. My girlfriend Candy respected my marriage, but with one failed marriage of her own and a cousin who recently passed away from Lupus; a similar disease, she naturally became protective. When she departed after praying for me, Anthony came in, "I don't trust you for invading my privacy and until you apologize, I have nothing to do with you!" For thirty-eight days he didn't have any physical contact with me and only spoke when necessary. Who does that? Anthony Devile' Rappt, that's who.

Dysfunction

I was diagnosed with Avascular Necrosis (Dead Bone) in my right shoulder, right before being released from the hospital. This routine X-ray after my hospitalization from an episode revealed the worst news ever. Needless to say, I was scheduled for surgery the next month. Meanwhile, I had to ask Anthony to consider going to marriage counseling and anger management. He turned to me in disgust, "For what? I'm good! You can go." With concern, Shannon looked at me, "Mom does he even care anymore?" I later found myself with my B.O.B (Battery Operated Boyfriend) mostly in the shower for all forms of relief. I felt cheated and so ridiculous, especially since I was married. I truly felt as though he was punishing me. I wondered, if I was taking care of myself, who or what is taking care of his self-gratification? One evening, he caught me taking care of myself and as I stepped out the shower, I was startled to see him sitting on the edge of our Jacuzzi. "May I finish what you've started?" Shocked, I replied, "Oh! He speaks! No thanks, I'm done." He jerked my aching arm, straddled me over his lap, and thrusted himself inside of me. When he was done, he looked at me with aggression in his eyes, "Never deny me. You know you needed this as much as I did." I was livid! *Did this N***a just rape me?* The crazy thing is, he's spoken of things such as this being legalized in Texas. Justifying his actions, he looked sternly in my eyes, "The man is the husband and if he takes it, it's because the wife wouldn't willingly give it up; therefore, it makes it legal because she can't press charges." I was pissed, "The devil is a liar and you have control issues. I hate what you just did to me." I looked at him in pure disgust, "Why would any man take a woman by force? That's rape, married or not!" Even after that, I had to square my shoulders back, prepare for surgery, and reassure Shannon that no matter what, since she made honor roll, I would make sure that she would have her thirteenth birthday party by the pool. Shannon would be allowed to invite as many friends as she liked.

Making Necessary Changes

I made a to do list to keep Shannon redirected, organized, and on time. I had all of her extra curriculum activities and church rehearsals on the list to keep her focused. Most importantly, I reassured her not to worry about my surgery or the arguments she'd heard her dad and I have. At age seven, Shannon was diagnosed with ADD which is an (Attention Deficit Disorder); however, before the diagnosis, she was tested as a gifted student because she would complete her work earlier than others and would later become disruptive during class. Her teacher described it as boredom and hyperactivity because she just couldn't seem to stay focused or stay still. Her little hands had to be busy at all times. We would clean up her room together and within an hour it would look like a Tsunami had just hit it and I just couldn't understand it. Her time management was off and she lost everything. In spite of it all, she may have been hyper, but she was never destructive. I had to quickly distinguish behavior verses diagnosis in order to separate the two. As time went on, I realized that she had challenges staying focused and concentrating, but I made sure she was disciplined accordingly. I firmly believed as the bible clearly said in Proverbs 13:24 that if you spared the rod, you would spoil the child. In knowing this, she was disciplined, but never abused. I just tried to raise her in the way she should go, so when she grew old, it wouldn't depart from her. (Proverbs 22:6). I cried, struggled, and prayed for her. I even took advice from people who "Did Not" have a child with this condition and that was the worst decision I could've made. Their advice sounded a little like this, "Spank her, take away privileges, keep her off sugary foods, and beverages, pray it away, it wasn't real, feed her beans and rice, no red meat, and absolutely no medication because it will make them sterile!" After a year of teacher/parent conferences, speaking with parents with diagnosed children, psychiatrist, monitoring my child, changing her diet, researching internet, viewing many hours of videos, praying and fasting... the reality remained that I undeniably knew that my little girl needed help and I was gonna give it to her. Before marrying Anthony, I educated him on my sickle cell, as well as her ADD, now ADHD. Just because she couldn't remember a few instructions he asked, "Is she retarded?" Livid, I addressed him, "Never ever call her that again. She's simply wired differently than others. She's very beautiful, intelligent, artistic, and ambitious. It's our jobs as her parents to teach her about God/salvation, love, support, as well as to provide and protect her. This world is ready to beat her down if we don't prepare her. You can't give her too much at once. If you break a paragraph down sentence by sentence ask if she comprehends it. Then, she can carry it through successfully. Be patient and compassionate with her as you would want someone to be with you." (Crickets). Now added on to my little angel comes this man with his dysfunction that he was in denial of. After realizing what was going on with my daughter, I made the necessary adjustments. However, dealing with Anthony, I didn't know how much more I could take. I knew Anthony suffers from anxiety, but I wondered while serving in the military and dodging bullets as well as firing them, should he have been diagnosed with PTSD (Post Traumatic Stress Disorder) and Bipolarism. He definitely exemplifies behaviors of both manic and depression characteristics. Since he continued to disregard my advice to eat natural sweets like fruits, he ended up being diagnosed with diabetes because he would constantly eat sugary candies. I guess being a physically fit man meant nothing. My mom always said, "A hard head makes a soft behind." That being said, he would have to stick his finger to check his blood sugar levels and I made sure that he ate better and took his insulin regardless of his actions because I couldn't stomach giving him those shots. Not to mention, he had poor vision because he wasn't taking care of himself and it whooping his butt.

2013: It's a Birthday Party

Shannon had finally turned thirteen with twenty-six children over for a swimming pool party. Although I had some parents to help me chaperone, some were reluctant and thought I was a bit extreme because I had a "No Harm Contract" for each parent to sign and date with their child's name printed before they stepped foot in our pool. (It's Called Necessary Safeguards) You see, Katie means protector of her loved ones and that was always my goal. I'll be "John Brown" as my dad used to say, if I didn't take the necessary precautions to avoid any later lawsuits. But back to the fun, I had nine booths of hula hoops, photo booth, go fish, dance off, dunking booth, table top games and more set ups to avoid the pool from being congested. We had sun screen, towels, first aid kits and instructions of Do's and Don'ts to follow. Sadly, there was only one other father there outside of Anthony. While Anthony was on the grill, he grilled hot dogs and burgers for the kids and a T-bone steak for himself. Outside of that, there were a total of about eight moms in all who helped prepare plates for the kids. I guess the saying is true, women really are the back bones of everything. Embarrassment gripped Shannon and I when Anthony yelled to the kids, "Hey, get off of my inflatable! And who got it out of the storage house?" I looked over at him, "Chill out, it was me who got it and it was an easy fix." I asked the kids to hand it over because Mr. Rappt didn't want anyone playing with it and they did, but their facial expression was like WOW! One young man nicely said, "We're so sorry Mr. Anthony, we didn't mean to offend you." Anthony was clearly embarrassed, "It's cool young man." I took the floater, deflated it and threw it in the storage. Anthony locked himself in our office for the remainder of the party and watched movies on his computer. I walked over and apologized to the kids and their mothers who overheard Anthony as they stood in disbelief on our porch. The only dad left at the grill took a plate and his kid's home. We then fed the kids, gave goodie bags, and distributed towels for them to dry off and change their clothes. Anthony refused to let them use our office because he claimed he was printing church programs; therefore, I sent them to Shannon's room, her bathroom, our guest bed rooms, and our master bath room. His outburst just killed the fun atmosphere of Shannon's party just as it had done many times in our marriage. Shannon was livid because her four friends decided to cancel their sleep over, but their mom's where kind enough to clean up before departing. Thank God! One seasoned mother grabbed my hand, "Keep Her Covered" which reminded me of Dr. See's comment (Keep Her Close). Not understanding why, I replied, "Yes ma'am." I knocked on Shannon's and Anthony's doors, "I'm going to deliver items the kids left behind. I'll be right back shortly." I had an uneasy feeling in my spirit, an urgency to get back home, so, I told my friend I would chat with her later. About thirty minutes later, I returned home to find Shannon still in her bathing suit screaming in a fetal position in the corner of her room. When I knelt down to pick her up, she yelled, "Ouch! Mama." Concerned, I asked, "What's wrong are you hurt?" She looked at me with tears flowing down her face, "Your husband beat me with a leather belt!" She pointed, "See!" She had red swollen welts all on her back, butt, and legs. Not to mention, some of her skin was broken with blood droplets appearing from the wounds. (Sign #3) I took a deep breath and comforted her, "No matter what you said or did, you didn't deserve this. This is abuse." As soon as I stood up and carefully placed her on the bed, I turned around to Anthony standing in the doorway breathing hard like an angry bull. "If you lie to your mama, I will beat your ass again." The momma bear in me stood up, "Oh no! I don't think so. Do you see the bruises you left on her? You've disciplined her before, but never like this." With a nervous look, Shannon said, "Yes he has. As a matter of fact, he waits until you leave, then I lie and try to cover it up at school. He tells me I better not say anything to you or else." She continued, "Thanks dad for ruining my party and causing my friends to leave and cancel my sleep over. You acted like a child over your floater." She turned her attention back to me. "Mama, when

I was getting ready to take off my swimsuit, he busted open my locked door, cursing, and started beating me until I fell to the floor covering my head. He doesn't realize how strong he is, especially when he's mad at me." I looked at him, "You are to never put your hands on her again. If I have to take her to the hospital, Social Services, DHR, and the police will be on the scenes for an investigation and your arrest. I will discipline her from now on." I looked back at Shannon, "How many times has this happened?" In disgust, I turned back to Anthony, "And why do you wait until I leave to discipline her Anthony?" He charged back, "I don't cater to a child that sassies me and you don't interrogate me woman. She ain't dead." I screamed, "And abusing her physically is ok?" As I soaked Shannon in Epson salt and mineral oil, her light skinned looked stripped and spotted with discoloration. I held back the tears as she described four other horrifying incidents as to how he had hurt her. I had no idea this had taken place right under my nose. Her opening up caused me to remember her not wanting to get undressed around me, the aches, and pains she said came from her monthly periods. It all made sense now. I vowed to her that those beatings and threats would never happen again. Not over my dead body.

Surgery May 24, 2013

I completed my lab, pre-op, and homework on Dr. Stella (The Surgeon) and turned in my Living Will with much prayer that no one would have to use it. In preparation for surgery, the nurse came in and took out a huge needle. I immediately shook my head, "No ma'am I've had my blood drawn with five tubes." With a concerned smile, she responded, "I know sugar pudding. Your white blood count is alarmingly low and we need to see if you're having a sickle cell crisis or if you're severely anemic." It's funny how you can find out any illness you may have through your blood. One hour later, the lab results determined that I needed a blood transfusion! The nurse went to find my husband in the waiting room, while I called my sister so that she could three way call my other family members to know the change of events and what to pray for. The meds were making me feel really relaxed and I needed Anthony to know about the changes immediately. Finally, when he came in, I asked him to pray over me and for the blood to be okay. His response was, "You must be losing blood from your head and those must be some good drugs making you talk cra cra. I ain't doing no such unnecessary thang." I was utterly shocked and all I could do was cry out to Jesus. He leaned over and looked into my eyes, "Text your holy-roller church family or better yet, put it on Facebook. You're nothing but a "Media Whore" seeking attention!" I pressed my emergency button and

71

asked the head nurse to have him escorted out by security. I then gave her a number and asked her to call my family to take care of Shannon until I decided what I was going to do once my surgery was over. Concerned, she took my cell phone away. It was clear to me that we were headed for divorce. *What was he so angry about?* My blood pressure went to the roof 159/115. As the nurse returned, she reassured me, "There's nothing to fear. The blood would be crossed matched. You're in the best surgeons' hands." Embarrassed, I answered her back, "No that's not it. My husband has really upset me and hurt me with his words of disbelief. So, I had him removed from my room." She knelt down close to my ear, pretending to tie my gown then spoke a profound word I'll never forget. "Some women stay because they don't think they deserve better, because they think it's the best they can do. It's not what you go through, it's WHO you go to. Testing before blessing!" I thanked the nurse for her words of wisdom before she went home from her 12-hour shift. Shortly thereafter, the blood arrived. I could tell the blood bag had frost on it, so I informed them, "Are ya'll nuts? I can't have ice cold blood put inside me. It will cause a full-blown crisis." Another hour delayed for them to figure out how to feed the blood through a separate (IV) in a warming machine. Once I received the blood, I informed the nurse that my tongue was swollen. Before I knew it, I had a severe reaction and started flopping on my bed like a fish out of water. I recalled eight people in my room before I blacked out or hmmm did they put me to sleep? The next day at about six o'clock, as they rolled me into the operating room, the doctor looked at me, "You gave us a scare young lady. I thought it would be best to postpone your surgery until you were stabilized. You were given compatible blood in which you had a severe reaction to. So, I ordered other alternative platelets to help elevate your anemia. Not to mention, your high blood pressure played a major factor in the delay. We're ready to rid you of your pain and I'm sure you are too. Keep calm and we'll take great care of you." He paused, "I'll send in the anesthesiologist, then we'll be on our way. Okie dokie." You've gotta love Southern slang. I began to worship and before I knew it, I woke up with Shannon rubbing my face with the back of her hand. She leaned over and whispered, "Wake up sleeping beauty. The doctor said you gave him a run for his money, but you did great mama." I wanted to hug her but all the bandages, tubes, and monitors were in the way. All I could do was offer her a weak smile because my throat was hurting from the breathing tube. I was comforted to see my family, my neighbor Robin, the pastor and first lady, along with a few church member's in that small room visiting me. They praised God, fluffed my pillow, put socks on my cold feet, showed me the fresh flowers/fruit basket, and balloons all to cheer me up. It struck a quiet praise in them and a few tears when I wrote on a napkin God Is Good, Thanks for everything. I told them that I needed some ice chips and a lobster dinner followed up with a smile!!! Due to me having another crisis, my brother asked Shannon to buzz the nurse. After the nurse checked on me, she cleared the room of my thoughtful guest, but my brother Edward asked for a private moment with me. It seemed as though my sisters didn't want him to right then, but he insisted. He asked, "How you feeling baby girl?" I nodded my head to let him know that I was okay. With a pissed expression, yet concerned look on his face, he continued, "You listen, I'll speak candidly. Baby girl, before you go home with that "Thug" of a husband, I want you to know that we heard how nasty and insensitive he spoke to you during our conference call." I was surprised because I forgot they were still on the call. My brother continued, "Regardless of the circumstances, you won't be talked to like that. Your dangerous high blood pressure, the non-compatible blood transfusion, and the complicated surgery you just endured is more than enough to deal with. Has that jerk ever put his hands on you?" I shook my head no! I lied! Although Anthony never hit me bare handed, pushing our office chair into my knee with his hand was the same as physical abuse. His temper was out of control. My grandmother always said, "Once a man hits you and you stay with him, look for another and another and all the lies, gifts, and sex to follow as his sick way of apologizing." She followed up with, "You don't miss your water until your well runs dry." My brother was a retired veteran from the Special Forces of thirty-three years with a black belt in Taekwondo and a zero tolerance for foolishness. I feared what he had done to my absent husband because Edward said, "That punk and I had a come to Jesus meeting and we now have an understanding. God frown's upon divorce. However, if he gives you a divorce take it or if you feel you need to divorce him after efforts and prayer, do it and call me. You can't possibly be happy. If he spoke to you like that and we heard it, he's done it before. Baby girl, you need to realize your worth." I missed hearing my beloved daddy calling me that. He would be so disappointed in the choice I'd made for a husband, the foolishness I've endured, as well as how unhappy I truly was. An hour later, Anthony came in with two dozen of colorful tulips, chocolates, tears, and a pitiful, "I'm sorry, please forgive me. You didn't deserve that." I asked, "Why?" He took a deep breath, "I ran out of my anxiety meds, I have to worry about all of the bills now, my mom has stage three cancer, and to be quite honest I'm jealous of your relationship with your family and church folks." I took a deep breath, "You need prayer and therapy" followed with me pressing the I.V drip for morphine and sleep. I've heard the excuses before, except my heart hurt for my mother in laws news. The next three months were very challenging and truly humbling being that my right hand was my dominant hand with limited mobility. I realized how I had taken the usage of my arms for granted, so, I quickly repented. Two weeks after having the eighteen staples removed from my Frankenstein looking incision, the bone specialist confirmed what my daughter said about me giving him a run for his money. He gave me the spill, "Once I opened up and removed the dead bone with two saws and a dead battery drill, I had the hardest task ever putting the titanium stint in your bone because it had marbleized. Perhaps in time the bone marrow will soften to slide the stint further down the bone in your arm. If I had tapped it down any further with the hammer, it would have shattered your bone and you would have lost your entire arm." I asked, "How can my bone marrow soften over time if its marbleized?" His response was, "Taking calcium tablets and careful therapy twice a week in house and in the clinic while being closely monitored by me, you should have full mobility of your arm, but just know NOTHING is guaranteed." After that, he wrote out another prescription for pain and completed the necessary forms for me to continue receiving short term disability. I was on my way to a painful recovery.

Anthony made sure that dinner was prepared and I was grateful for his help. So, I overlooked all of the dust bunnies that were forming because I understood that their clean was definitely not my clean. Shannon helped me keep my arm dry as I showered, dressed me, and folded all the laundry. After thirty days I was getting cabin fever because I missed work, church, and my independence. So, to keep occupied during that time of boredom and depression, I read half the bible, two novels, the newspapers, and checked out several self-help books from the local library. Being that I was an avid reader, this was so beneficial for me and my growth. Anthony picked up CD's from my church so that I could hear the word preached. He even made sure Shannon was driven to after school activities and all rehearsals at church. He complained about the bills, but after we were given the green light to become intimate, he became nice again, he became the man I fell in love with. It were as if he had split personalities because his attitude changed like the weather. Bedtime was the worse because the pain from the surgery kept me awake even with six pillows surrounding me for support. Not to mention, my sleep was forever broken with Anthony's work schedule because he would come to bed around 4:00 or 6:00 a.m., from watching T.V or on his computer. Within five minutes he would be snoring and I hated it because the snoring was a result of his refusal to use his sleep apnea machine. He would have frequent nightmares, not to mention he would talk in his sleep. Sleeping in the same bedroom with him irritated my sleep. I told him if he ever said the wrong thing in his sleep, I would pour hot sauce down his throat. This particular night I was very drowsy from my medication and comfortably lying on my back when he started kicking with his unmanicured toe nails and shouting from a horrible apparent violent nightmare, "No, I don't want to go there." When I tapped his arm, he turned over, swung, and punched me right in my incision with a closed fist. I screamed with tears flowing down my face. With no concern, he smacked his lips, wiped the sweat off of his forehead, and rolled over. I yelled, "Anthony wake up! You just punched me in my arm." He scoffed, "What do want me to do about it? You know I was dreaming. It was an accident. Don't be a cry baby." If looks could kill, I would have been cashing in his life insurance policy for $100,000. I snatched the covers off of him and wobbled to the bathroom to discover one of the staples had popped and was now dripping blood. I cleaned and bandaged it, then went into the guest bedroom. I wondered to myself, *when will the real Anthony Rappt show up?* Sadly, it was time for therapy and boy did I dread it because it made me cry. The pain was just unbearable. I made an emergency appointment with my physician and he saw me right away.

He took another x-ray and with great concern, he looked at me, "I'm so sorry but this surgery didn't take. The stint never moved down as I had hoped. It's still sticking out an inch and a half. That's why your right arm can't go over your head." Baffled, I decided it was best to get a second opinion. On the way out, I looked back at the doctor, "Have a blessed day." Outside of this horrible news, I felt like I had to walk on egg shells around Anthony because I didn't know what would set him off. Being that he was considered immediate family and of course my husband, I decided to respectfully share the news with him, but after his comment, I wish that I would've went to my family who actually cared instead. I walked over to him, "I just left work to fill out more paper work—" Before I could finish my sentence, he cut me off, "Thank you Jesus the doctor released you back to work. Now you can take over full payments of your bills rather than some of them with that pitiful Aetna check." My brows creased, "I hate to be the bearer of bad news, but I'm scheduled for another surgery in three months. I won't be returning to work just now because the first surgery failed." His nostrils flared, "Really, well there seems to be a lot of that going on around here." Baffled, I shook my head, "It's not my fault. I need your support." I pulled myself together after his dramatic exit and searched the wiregrass for another physician with no success. Due to liability, no other physician wanted to correct another physician's unsuccessful surgery. I later found an orthopedic surgeon that would consider correcting the problem, but it would have to be one year later. He wouldn't even view the X-rays. During this time, as I searched for a surgeon, eight other doctors gave me the same answer while I suffered unnecessarily. I had no choice but to return to this doctor, I now viewed as the "Butcher." He explained that he was surprised to learn that I had went to one of his colleagues. Taken back, my eyes grew wide, "What did you expect me to do after you told me that my arm was stuck? You explained that the x-ray revealed that the stint was sticking an inch and a half out of my bone? Therapy would have never been successful." I took a deep breath, "Thanks to you, my arm is worse than when I first came to you. Although I was in pain before this surgery, at least I had full mobility." He apologized, "You were one of three cases that kept me awake because I knew I would have to redo the surgery to save your arm." I shook my head, "Well that's about $300,000.00 total huh? I'm glad I have my medical coverage form in the mail and thank God my husband also has high secondary insurance so that we don't have to pay out of pocket." He obviously became offended and lashed back, "Mrs. Rappt, if I wanted to become rich, I would practice in another state or country." I felt bad for going off and looked at him with apologetic eyes, "I'm sorry if I offended you. I'm truly afraid

80

of going under the knife with you again, but no one else will touch me. The streets talk Doc." He smiled, "I can assure you that the next surgery will work if you'll give me the chance. You won't regret your decision." Then he gave me an oil painting of baby Jesus. The sad part is the gift was for one of his previous nurses who abruptly quit over the holiday due to the major lawsuits he had on his end. Although I thought it to be a rebound gift, I smiled, "Thank you."

Ex-Girlfriend

I spoke with my supervisor and the medical leave department to complete my (Out Process) forms due to surgery. This would guarantee continued income for me and that my job would be there when I returned from medical leave. Before leaving, they all gave me their God speed well wishes. Too bad I couldn't get that from my own husband and something just didn't feel right. I wondered if I needed to contact an investigator about the secret phone calls Anthony continued to make on company time to his ex-girlfriend. It's crazy because I had given him many opportunities to be truthful, but he continued to deny everything. I remember how he would talk about his co-workers cheating on their wives, not helping with chores, and how they picked on him for being faithful and helping around the house. OLD HYPOCRITE!!!!! A few days later while having my car detailed, the cleaner guy found a hidden receipt in the corner of the car. I had a cousin's friend to check on the frequently used number 555-222-3335 with the name Bethany Odam (His Ex-Girlfriend) I was confused, *if he wanted her so bad, why didn't he propose to her?* I overheard him on the speaker phone and realized that he was talking to his sister. I listened closely as she continued, "I got some tea to spill." He replied, "Spill it." She continued, "You need to get to momma's house and break up with your side chic girlfriend and close that chapter of your life." I abruptly walked into the office so that his sisters could hear me, "Stop stirring the pot. This isn't funny and Anthony doesn't need any encouragement to be a part of (His Ex) "Thirsty" drama." Just say, I lost respect for them instantly for being (Petty). We walked out of the office and went into our bedroom while he continued to talk to his sister, "Besides, I'm in love with Katie. She's my wife." As he hung up his house phone, I found out that this chic (His Ex) flew in from Florida to his mom's house begging her to convince him not to marry me, but that was too late, I'm Mrs. Rappt now. Apparently, she felt that she deserved him; not me. As we sat in his bedroom, I folded my arms, "Anthony call your ex now." At first, he seemed a bit agitated, but as I sat on the bed, he made the call. After she answered I felt sorry for her. He winked at me and took a deep breath, "Bethany, I need for you to leave my mom's house and accept the fact that it's over and that I've moved on." Boom, without him knowing, it was clear that the numbers from the cleaners matched. It was confirmed that he had been calling his ex. As for her, I would never be so desperate for a man and act so foolish, but for him, I'm glad that he handled that issue because it wasn't for me to put her in her place, it was his. That was his past and to avoid disrespecting our future, him addressing what had just happened was absolutely necessary. But apparently, I was wrong. I thought to myself, *He's been caught calling her with months of data to prove it, it clearly show's he's not over her after all.* Because of Anthony's infidelity, I began to develop low self-esteem and began to question myself as a woman and a wife. I felt that he needed emotional attention from one of my self-help books because it could surely provide that for him. Regardless of the fact, I prepared his favorite meal with a no sugar peach cobbler with lite whip cream topped off with a nonalcoholic beer to avoid extra calories not interfere with his high blood pressure meds and diabetes. I had a bubble bath drawn for him with heated warming lavender oil to create a calming environment. Not to mention, I sacrificed a bill to purchase his favorite cologne. The house was immaculate and I had Shannon to spend the night with her granny. I then showered, put on my white satin teddy, and pinned up my curly hair. He was stunned when he walked through the door with a pleasant smile on his face, "What's all this?" We enjoyed our meal with no conversation of bills stacking up, my forthcoming surgery, his phone calls to his side chic, his snoring, or our different faiths. Just sweet nothings and how we needed to communicate better with understanding, love, and respect. We sincerely apologized to one another and enjoyed our sweet desserts. This was my answered prayer... peace in my HOME. The devil didn't win that battle. POW!!! He gets a black eye in Jesus name.

August 28th 2014/2nd Surgery

By now, I knew the drill of everything! The only difference was that this surgery was at a different hospital. I alerted all of my prayer warriors so they could begin interceding on my behalf. When it came to my blood type, I made sure they gave me B Positive unfrozen for the blood transfusion, then I put the surgeon in God's hands. The surgery would be quick and pain free because I had an increased amount of meds in my nerve block medication. They ran a small needle like tubing in my neck, inserted a catheter, a breathing tube for oxygen, connected me to the blood pressure monitor, gave an (IV) intravenous therapy with meds, followed by a fluid drainage tube from my arm, and a blood transfusion (IV). Just say, I looked like an alien with tentacles hanging out of me. Sadly, it bothered Shannon to see me like that and it really hurt because the first time she saw me, she screamed, but this time the staff was aware, attentive, and seemingly more knowledgeable to avoid frightening her. It was this "quack" of a doctor that made me skeptical though. So, before surgery I hummed a tune to a praise song to calm myself. Then, shortly thereafter, a wonderful nurse by the name of Joy came in to check my vitals and sang with me. The funny thing is that I had seen her a few times before at my church. I reached for her hand with gratitude, prayed for God's covering and quickly read Psalm 91. The nurse gave a reassuring smile as she walked out to inform the anesthesiologist that we were ready. He then walked in with a joyful smile, "Ma'am it's just you and I in here for now." I returned a smile, "That's what you think son, let's do this." After surgery, I woke up in excruciating pain in my back and chest known as (Acute Chest Syndrome). Just say this pain was different. I was having another sickle cell crisis, a distinct feeling, I knew all too well. I didn't speak to anyone in my room; however, myself and those who were well educated about this autoimmune disease that I hated moved hastily not missing a beat. I pressed the button while Marie turned my oxygen up to 3.0, Anthony ran to get the doctor, Shannon propped up my pillows and put her ear to my mouth to find out where I hurt, and my momma went into her war room (The Bathroom) to pray. During a sickle cell crisis, it requires immediate medical attention due to the organs being attacked without oxygen or sufficient blood. I just so happened to already be at the right place at the right time (The Hospital) Only God could see to that! I was required to remain hospitalized for another week and of course I hated it because I just wanted to go home. When the doctor made his rounds, he walked in confidently, "Mrs. Rappt, I must say, I was very pleased with the surgery. You'll need continuous therapy as it is key to a successful recovery. I needed some energy laying there in that hospital, so, I secretly had my oldest sister Leslie drive from ATL to make me some Dr. Sees soup and tea. I just hated that Marie couldn't make it, but she had to teach a Science class. For weeks, I couldn't do anything but rest, depend on my little nurse Shannon, and pray that Anthony would take our vows seriously. You know the part I'm talking about (Through Sickness & Health). Oddly, he was unusually quiet as he cared for me and I didn't know how to take that. He said that he slept in our guest bed room because he didn't want to make the mistake of hitting me during nightmares that he frequently had. By the fourth week, I started regaining my strength but having to wear this huge cushioned black arm sling for three more weeks was a challenge. Not to mention getting dressed and enjoying a comfortable night's sleep. I couldn't scratch the top of my head, unless I bent my neck to do so (Annoying). I couldn't write my name or wipe my backside. God forbid if I ever got arrested and the Po Po tried to handcuff my hands behind my back; it would literally break my arm. This surgery was a nightmare and therapy made me cry and scream. To avoid focusing on the pain, I began to focus on what I could do instead. I began taking prescribed medication like candy to reduce the pain and in doing so, it caused constant constipation which required me to take laxatives for regular bowel movements. Just say that many compared constipation to natural birth. One week later, therapy began. The pain was excruciating as I walked my fingertips up the wooden ladder mounted to the wall during physical therapy. It was my greatest challenge. Although, I made it to thirty on the ladder, my goal was forty, but for some odd reason, my arm simply wouldn't extend straight enough. The pain was so bad that I was eating medication for breakfast to wake up, snacking on them to try to function, and eating them for dinner to sleep without pain. I stopped praying, reading, drawing, being a mother, and a wife. Depression came in and kidnapped every good emotion I had that would cause me to care about anything or anyone and I hated that. The feelings of unworthiness seemed to affect my entire household and lifestyle. Sadly, I had become my mother, someone I promised myself that I would never become. Shannon's grades plummeted a whole letter grade and I'm pretty sure my behavior played a major role in that and Anthony not making sure that she took her ADHD meds made matters even worse. She missed too many rehearsals to participate in dance, the garbage can was full of fast food bags, the house had so many dust bunnies, you'd think it was Easter. Laundry was on our office couch and needed folding, unopened mail was stacked high on the counter, and I clearly ignored the bible disk on my dresser. I just didn't care anymore. Besides, Anthony and I were like two ship's sailing by with whispers of a few words. I was so agitated that I couldn't sleep causing me to feel like a zombie and he stopped rubbing my arm and helping me with therapy. You would think that was enough, but then came the frequent nightmares of a young girl running for help without a face. Whenever I woke up on Sundays, I would hear Shannon and Anthony wrestling, knocking furniture over, and shouting, "1, 2, 3, ding ding ding I win!" I was too medicated, in too much pain, too depressed, or all three at once to tell them to be quiet. I wished that they would've just sat down and played a board or a computer game. I screamed within, "STOP IT!!!" In addition to everything else, I never felt good about them wrestling simply because he was so much stronger than she was. I feared that something would break or worse; he would grab her body parts accidently. When he would come to check on me, he would be surprised if I were sitting up. Frustrated, I looked over at him, "STOP IT NOW!!" His brows met, "What's the problem? That's our fun way of bonding." I snapped, "Ya'll need to bond together and clean this filthy house." He fired back, "You're so ungrateful and selfish. Frankly, I think you're jealous and addicted to those pain killers. You've become my mom and yours all in one." That hard and painful reality shook me to the core. He was right and I needed immediate spiritual surgery for complete deliverance. I randomly grabbed one of the disks from my dresser to listen to the watch night service I had previously missed in preparation for surgery with my head phones on and the volume on high. Sadly, my attitude started to reflect that which Shannon's Psychologist had talked with her about. My thinking was truly stinking. Her attitude was off the charts and so was mine. After hearing our anointed praise team sister's in a unified harmonized voice, I then heard the pastor say, "Excuse me while I tell you the truth! If God will bring you to it, He will bring you through it. Look at your neighbor and say, 'Won't He do it." Please be seated in the presence of the Lord and be so kind to turn your Bibles with me to Jonah 1: 1-17." The message spoke directly to me. Paraphrased, it went a little like this, "When you're disobedient, get ready to go through tough times." When I taught young children, I had a saying, *when you get what you get and don't pitch a fit.* Just as Jonah, I heard God say, "Go to" instead I ran from the thing He was directing me to. Just as Jonah got swallowed up by the huge fish, I suddenly realized I was being swallowed up by life. I had to pray my way through these storms because they didn't seem to want to let up. Repentance, repentance, here I come. I realized that I had to go through the process and no longer run from God, my prayer life, assembling myself with believers, reading, fasting, praying, and I had to stop allowing the spirit of depression take over my life. I realized that it was okay to be angry, but sin not. Instead of fervently praying and surrendering my marriage to God, I allowed the enemy to use me to argue with a man who clearly needed deliverance as head of his household. I had to be honest with myself in order for me to grow in Christ. I realized and accepted the fact that I had neglected my family, needed an intimate relationship with God and for Him to keep me in good standing so that I wouldn't go astray. To be honest, I had no choice but to trust Him to fix my heart and my broken spirit. Reality was that I hated that I depended more on prescription drugs than I did God. When I finally came to that realization, instantly as a backslider, I became remarried to God; however, remaining married to my earthly husband was going to be a joint effort. I know God heard my prayers because immediately a darkness was lifted from me and I desired change within to be redeemed for another chance at life. I stopped taking my meds for the wrong reasons and called for a family meeting. As we sat there, I looked both Shannon and Anthony in their eyes, "I'm sorry for my emotional detachment. I will never check out on either of you again. From this day forward, I'm fighting for this family. I've recognized that I was being deceived by the enemy, but no more. I promise to do better. It would warm my heart if we could all be on one accord. I would love for us to be kind, forgiving, loving, and have better communication with each other to make that happen." We had an open discussion of what made us unhappy and suggestions to make our house a home of harmony and peace. Shannon and I opened every window, door, and loudly commanded Satan and his demons to get out of our house. I even anointed the house with blessed oil. I thought Anthony would participate in praying and anointing our home, but he felt that agreeing to get along was enough participation. Division!!! How can two walk together lest they agree is what my granny used to say. We later cried and prayed together, topped with forgiveness, and respectfully put forth an effort to honor one another's request. Although apprehensive, Shannon shared her first request, "I just wish you and dad would stop arguing and that dad would stop being so mean with his words and be more supportive of my activities." I turned to Anthony, "I think we need marriage counseling and anger management classes instead of suffering in silence." He leaned back, "And I need for you to let me wear the pants and be the head of this household. In other words, I need for you to take a few seats." (Crickets) Hours later, Anthony and I discussed the other concerns we had privately. We just didn't feel Shannon's presence was necessary for that. Anthony leaned back, "Kay, I freaked out about the finances and I shouldn't have taken it out on you." I took a deep breath, "Anthony, were unequally yoked. You wouldn't even help me anoint the house." He rubbed his forehead, "Baby steps Tink. I'm trying. I know we're unhappy and yes we've got work to do to turn this thing around." I smiled, "Well, are you willing to put in the work?" He reached for my hand, "I wouldn't have said it, if I wasn't." I fumbled my ring around my finger, "Ok let's work it out." The next week, my doctor had his nurse to call me after cancelling all of my therapy sessions for an explanation. Needless to say, Anthony and I got there right away. He had his long curly red hair in a man bun on top of his head. (Yuk) It was crazy because he said the weirdest thing in front of us and I quote, "I Love You!" We glanced at each other as he continued, "I'm not going to beat around the bush uh um I... I..." At the same time, we shot back, "Spit it out already." He sat down on his stool, "I'm sending you to

UAB for corrective surgery! I called a friend who is top of the line. You're the toughest case I've ever had in twenty years. Katie, I want you to have at least 90% usage of your arm. That bone of yours really gave me a run for my mon...." Anthony was livid, "Shut Up!!!! Shut the hell up. Don't ever tell my wife that you love her or address her by her first name. You said she was in good hands. You said that you were the best. You asked us to give you another chance and that we could trust you. Now you wanna sit here and say she gave you a run for your money. This my wife's life you screwing with. You ain't sending her no damn where. We'll get our own real surgeon at UAB and you'll be hearing from our attorney idiot." Wow!!! My husband finally stood up for me, but knowing that a third surgery was required shocked me to the core. We asked for the x-ray from the second shoulder replacement and we were informed that the previous before and after x-ray's were no longer in the office; however, they could be requested at the hospital where the surgery took place. We then requested the disk, took it home for viewing, and discovered that it only had my first surgery x-rays on it from the rod sticking out of my arm. Before closing of business, we went back to my doctor's office. Once again, we were lied to with the explanation of his absence. "I'm sorry, he's in surgery and he would have to be present to authorize the releasing of your x-ray. I do apologize, but

we wouldn't have it in this office. We don't store disk here."
Frustrated that we were given the run around, Anthony
spoke up, "This dickweed is hiding something." The next
morning, I saw my primary physician and explained
everything. He gave us one particular reference, "Please
allow me to recommend an Orthopedic Surgeon at another
hospital who works with a Hematologist just in case you
have to have another blood transfusion. The hospital I'm
referring you to has a state-of-the-art unit for blood." Shortly
thereafter, the doctor had his nurse call to encourage me not
to worry about my unfound x-ray disks because they would
recapture them to see how to resolve the pain. Needless to
say, after the X-Rays were redone, they discovered more
issues.

My 3rd Surgery

My replacement was scheduled for Nov 10, 2014. Together,
we made several doctor trips to an Orthopedic that was
flown in from Italy, who initially revealed that the pain was
due to my entire shoulder being "dislocated." With concern
he sat down and began speaking in his strong accent, "Your
arm was only attached by muscle and tissue. That's probably
why you never received your x-rays. Ide'at." The doctor was
even the more shocked that the therapy didn't cause more
damage. He continued, "The physical therapy only made

everything worse." *No wonder I was uncomfortable. It was a miracle that I was able to tolerate the constant severe pain.* Anthony looked over at me, "Oh, that explains why you were popping pills like candy." I was placed in a tight sling with instructions not to use my arm and to keep it in a hugging position around my waist until after the third and final surgery. The only time I could take it off was in the shower. During my doctor's visit, he explained, "Mrs. Rappt, this is going to be a very complicated surgery to remove the titanium rod and replace it with a reasonable size without shattering your arm." While there, I had to have a few labs that later revealed that I had developed millions of antibodies due to receiving the wrong blood type during the transfusion. With this new information, the doctor knew that they would need to cross match my blood, bank my blood, or consider a stem cell transplant by using my sibling's bone marrow since I couldn't receive blood from anyone outside of my family, not even universal blood (O or AB-Blood Type). The nurse briefed us on pre-op paper work, insurance, diets, do's and don'ts, more lab, and a current living will. The doctor's eyes grew wide as he explained, "Mrs. Rappt, your shoulder was hanging on by muscles and tissue. I honestly don't know how you endured so much pain, trauma, or stress, but we're gonna to make it better." I was baffled. Once again minor adjustments had to be made to take care of Shannon, mom, and my own household issues in a darn sling for six months yet for a third shoulder replacement. For the next couple of months until my surgery, I had to really take it easy. During that time, Shannon was suspended from school for fighting. She walked in not knowing what I was going to say, "Momma, I can explain. I was being bullied about my long legs, this grey patch of hair in the center of my head, and my wild curly hair." I just wish I could've managed her locks better professionally, but I just couldn't afford it at the time and it hurt knowing that kids could be so cruel. No one wants their child to be bullied about their hair or anything else. But I had to address the fight. I listened as she continued to explain, "Mom, I didn't provoke her or throw the first punch. I even tried to talk it over, but she wouldn't stop. She wouldn't stop teasing me about you having to trade in your dream car, or me having to downgrade with my phone." She paused, "Momma, that was embarrassing." In Mudea's voice I looked at her, "Girl, people gone talk regardless of how good or bad you are and you can't stop that. Either you gone believe who they say you are or who God says you are, but you can't do both. You responding only gave them ammunition. You remember that; you hear me? God said you are fearfully and wonderfully made. You can find that in Psalms 139:14. Oh, and that phone of yours is just stuff." She shook her head, "Mama I'm sorry. I can care less about what she said about me. I'm confident in who I am and Who's I am." As she continued to explain everything that happened and who was involved, it broke my heart to learn that one of the young ladies from our church who knew of our physical and financial struggles was involved. That explains why she became defensive. I took a deep breath, "Now you have a week's worth of zeros to make up for the poor decision you made. You've gotta pick your battles honey. There are always consequences to our choices. You stood up for what you believed in and now I'm standing up for what I believe in." As I turned to walk away, I looked back. "By the way, you're grounded for a month." Apparently, Anthony was eavesdropping because he stood from afar with his arms folded and had his say, "She need a beat down and both of ya'll self-proclaimed preachers need to hush with all of them quotes." I looked at Shannon, "See baby girl, this is a primary example of what I mean by pick your battles. This one is certainly not worth fighting. Let's eat dinner." Anthony left for work without an embrace, kiss, or a good bye. *Apparently, the contract we signed was soon forgotten.*

Karma

Since it was a Thursday/laundry day, I decided to get my hands and mind busy. I knew that minor adjustments had to be made to assist Shannon with time management and organization skills; however, seeing her garments turned inside out, irritated me to no end. It also worked my nerves when Anthony would leave hard candy and money inside his pockets. To make matters worse, I detected a tightly folded form inside of Anthony's tiny tight jean pocket. After advancing to my new DEA skills, I walked into my bathroom, locked the door, and carefully opened the paper. I discovered two pages of Verizon invoices with over thirty in-coming and out-going calls to 555-222-3335 to the infamous Ms. Bethany Odam (His Ex). I saw red and hell rose up inside of me prompting me to pose as "KARMA" myself. I put hair remover inside his shampoo bottle, scrubbed his toothbrush inside our toilet, urinated in his sweet tea container, used Shannon's special woman sauce in his spaghetti, put pin holes in his inflatable, ex-Lax in his no sugar chocolate brownies, threw away his charge cord, and finally, I sugared his gas tank. Apparently, I had been watching way too many movies for my devious inspirations. I was livid and that resulted in my resorting back to an I don't care attitude. I had to be careful as to how I handled this cheating jerk.

(Please note that my decisions were ungodly and I regret each one of them. But the purpose of sharing the decisions I made is to let every reader know how mean

spirited and bitter one can become when we seek out revenge instead of letting God fight our battles no matter how saved or not. Two wrongs don't make a right.)

I was inclined to call Human Resources and anonymously mail all of the phone records and invoices as proof to show that he was using company time to call her, but that meant I would risk him getting fired, then we'd all be homeless. I deliberately allowed his clothes to remain in the washer wet to sour; however, when he asked me about his laundry, I lied. Whenever he wanted to be intimate, I lied even the more to say I was in severe pain or medicated too much to perform. I despised him, I didn't respect him, nor did I like him, and slowly but surely, I was falling out of love with him. He would pick fights as a form of punishment and complained about having to work, cook, clean, take care of himself, pay bills, take care of the yard, and us/we his family day in and day out. He complained about how he didn't want cereal boxes or milk jugs to be placed inside of our kitchen garbage to reserve space. He didn't even want us to drink his Grapefruit juice. He consistently yelled at us for not replacing water bottles in the refrigerator and using his computer. If I quit my job or if they fired me, I would not like being Mrs. Homemaker Rappt. Who did he think he was? I had been working too? To avoid his extra attitude, I stayed away for extra hours to take care of my mother, I volunteered at church, and spent extra time with Shannon, but even during that time, her attitude, not cleaning her room, and her not keeping up with her frequent chores became a thorn in my flesh. He was bringing the worst out of me and I didn't like who I was becoming. Once again, I allowed the devil to use me. My friends stopped visiting because Anthony would air out our dirty laundry, get into debates about politics, religion, and police brutality. He was ashamed to be black himself! He only watched certain movies because I wouldn't shut up about supporting our own. He constantly spoke of how he felt young men with saggy pants should be jailed then raped. I really thought he had lost his mind when he said his televisions appeared to him at night to show him futuristic occurrences. He was an embarrassment to me and the entire black race. He really needed therapy, meds, prayer, and total deliverance. I believe trauma from his childhood, fighting over seas, and the little girl burning in the fire played a major role in him becoming so bitter and angry and we were his targets. Knowing this made it vital to fully recover from my last and final surgery, go back to work, and work on the spiritual attacks we were experiencing or we would be defeated.

Living Will

On Monday February 10, 2015, my surgery was delayed three hours to assure that my blood type would be properly cross matched. The doctor made sure that I would be lightly medicated for the three-and-a-half-hour ride to avoid stress. Taking the necessary precautions would eliminate any possible sickle cell crisis due to stress. That worked for me because I didn't have to say a word to Mr. Cheat and he didn't have to say anything to me. Just say, it was a peaceful ride. Finally, I arrived to the hospital and was assigned a room. As I adjusted myself in the bed, Justice, the head nurse came in. At my request, she sang me an old hymn, anointed my head, and shoulder with prayer oil and smiled. "Baby, don't you worry. You're surrounded by nothing but believers. We're all filled with the Holy Spirit from the Hematologist that's matching your blood to the Anesthesiologist and the nurses Michael, Hope, Joy and Miracle, not to mention your surgeon Dr. Bonce' who was once a Chaplin in the military who believed that he could heal the body in more ways than one. Just say, God takes the lead with this crew. We don't hide who we are or Who's we are. You're in God's hands darling. When you wake up, I'll be by your bedside, so don't fear because God didn't give you that spirit, but He gave you and I spirit of power, love and of sound mind." With a feeling of relief, I smiled, "Thank you Jesus." I finally closed my eyes for the best sleep ever. When I woke up there was a poster board that was signed by all of my caregivers. It read: *It's not a sin to be sick, your illness is not your identity and your character is not your chemistry* by Pastor Rick. With just me and my Heavenly Father alone in the room, I looked up, "Thank you for waking me up with a praise on my mind. Thank you for this being a successful surgery and my last. Please forgive me for all intentional sins committed against my husband. Lord, if it's Your will, please restore, renew, refresh, revive, and return all that was lost in my marriage. Change me and create in me a clean heart and renew the right spirit within me. Not my will but Your will be done." As I laid in that hospital bed looking like a tentacle tubed octopus, I rededicated my life to God yet again. The good thing is that I wasn't in pain, but I was very sore and uncomfortable. Literally, nurses rotated rounds for forty-eight hours to help get me up and going. After signing the release forms, Anthony looked over at me, "Let's go home. I heard you were a champ." He kissed me on the forehead, "Here we go again." With confidence, I smiled, "Yea for better, for worse, for richer, for poorer, in sickness and in health til death do us part." (Crickets) I arrived home to Shannon waiting in my bedroom with a dozen of red roses. She smiled, "I know you like tulips but these smell so sweet. They reminded me of you." I returned a smile, "How so?" She walked towards me, "They're pretty, sweet smelling, and full of painful thorns that needs to be pruned." Well, well, well. Out of mouths of babes. She placed them in a large crystal vase and gave me a long tight hug that hurt and whispered, "I'm so glad your back home to make things better again!" I softly hugged her with tears in my eyes, "I will Shugga." Reality is, that statement worried me. With great concern, I winked, "We'll talk alone tomorrow." While I was gone, Anthony had turned our guest bedroom into a man-cave. He had his own laptop, screen T.V, a microwave, a fridge, a cell charger, snacks, and sports décor all over the wall. I looked at him, "Why do you need a man cave?" He scoffed, "I need space. Oh, and time alone away from work and from you." It just rolled off his tongue as if I understood, as if I wouldn't care, as if it wouldn't have hurt me. I looked at him, "You act like you're single in a college dorm." (Crickets) Regardless of his insensitive statement, I didn't show any emotion. I shook my head, walked away, and tried to refocus my thoughts to the positive side of things. The house was immaculate, the refrigerator and cabinets stocked, fresh linens on the beds, the lawn was manicured, and all of the laundry was completed. Even Shannon's room was well organized and spotless. The aroma of the house smelled of lavender, but something wasn't right in my home. My spirit just couldn't shake it. I didn't want to go straight to bed, so I ate some home-made vegetable soup and sipped on hot tea with lemon while soaking in the sun on our back porch to a view of our clean pool. I looked up, "Lord please give me clarity, healing, and peace." It was sunny, yet chilly, so later that evening, I had them to set me up in my bed. After Shannon and I worked on some puzzles for an hour, I kissed her good night. Anthony closed my door with a faint smile, "Get some rest. You're gonna need it!" That left me baffled. When I woke up, I was in pain but it was tolerated enough for Aleve tablets. There's a distinct difference between sickle cell pain and any other pains that I've ever felt. Shannon found the bell that our announcer used during our wedding next to my bed. It brought tears to my eyes as I rang the bell for help and as usual, my little princess came immediately. "How can I help you madam?" I smiled, "Help mama to get to the bathroom so that I can take a bath and put on some fresh clothes." When she helped me up, I looked over at her, "Where's your daddy?" She smiled, "He's still in his cave." As I got undressed, Shannon respected me enough to turn away when I sat in our extra-large garden tub. When it was time for my other follow-up appointment, I guess Anthony didn't forget about his clothes souring in the washer, so in turn he pretended to forget the date of my appointment at UAB and let me drive three and a half hours by myself.

Code Talk

As we sang, Shannon's beautiful sopranos voice soothed my heart and brought back sweet memories of us together at our churches Mother's/Daughter's tea outing. She gently rubbed my back while my arm was propped under a folded towel and bent down near my ear and spoke in Spanish, "Mama' tengo un amigo que esta' en problemas en casa. Ella esta' avergonzada y si ella dice l o que esta' pasando, puede separa a see familia. Que' deberia decircle que. Haga? Siella esta', siendo lastimada, necesita decirle a alguien en quien confie que la ayude, de inmediato. Shannon, esta's bien? (Silencio) es para un, amigo mama... Gracias." (Translation) "Mom, I have a friend who's in trouble at home and she's embarrassed. If she tells what's happening, it may break up the family. What should I tell her to do? If she's being harmed, she needs to tell someone she trusts to help her immediately." Confused, I answered her, "Shannon, are you ok?" (Silence) "Momma, it's for a friend mom." Meanwhile, Anthony called us into the living room for a family meeting. She and I sat together holding hands and listened to his written contract. *As the man of this house, I am the Head and*

105

take that position back 100%. The fourth of July, we're having a merged family party. Since I'm the only one working with a paycheck, I will decide what we buy down to the toilet paper. Wife, you ain't gonna like being home-maker Rappt, but you better get used to it. Shannon, since your mama won't let me raise you the way I should as your daddy, you answer to her for everything, all expenses too. Both of you knock on my caveman door before coming in. Meeting is Adjourned! After he read his contract, we looked at each other with bucked eyes and our mouths hanging to the floor. As he attempted to walk out of the room without asking if we had any questions or concerns, I tried to get up fast and give him a piece of my mind starting with, "Who in the hell do you think you are?" But Shannon stopped me, "Mama let it go and let God fight your battles." Once again, out of mouths of babes. Finally, after he left the room, I discussed my living will with Shannon. I placed my hand on her hand, "Baby, if anything happens to me, your auntie, my authorized sister Marie and mom will be your guardians and you'll live with them since Anthony said he wouldn't honor my request for you to attend our church." I took a deep breath, "He told me to take you to them since he couldn't raise you the way he wanted if I died. I'm sorry to get you involved in our adult issues, but I need for you to understand that he's mad with me not you sweetheart." With downward eyes, she replied,

"I don't think I ever want to get married momma!" (SMH) She and I later snuggled in my king size bed, watched movies, and laughed, until we heard Anthony's door slam to his man cave and listened as he blasted his television while he watched wrestling. (So Sad) That night Shannon wet the bed and I had nightmares of a huge hairy hand with long finger nails reaching for her as she stood in front of her bathroom mirror. Not to mention, I too was embraced by this monster. It's crazy because we both woke up gasping for air and our hearts pounding. I reached over to comfort her, "Baby, it's okay. I'm right here." She took a long shower as I dry vacuumed the mattress and put fresh linens on the bed. "Baby, this is our little secret, no worries." She lowered her head, "I must've drank too much water and was probably dreaming about swimming." Whatever it was, it made her pee to bed. I knew it was a sign of digression and I had to find the source. When she finally drifted back off to sleep, I went into my war closet knowing that I was in a spiritual warfare. I laid prostrate on my face asking God to reveal to me what I was dealing with, no matter how painful or ugly it was. I needed for God to prepare me to know what to do. As I waited on God for an answer, I prayed for forgiveness. I needed for God to give me a clean heart and renew the right spirit within me. I couldn't afford to miss Him (God) because something wasn't right. The next morning, I took Shannon

107

to our favorite spot, the park. There, she was able to openly share in a calm, safe, beautiful environment all of her fears and concerns without distractions. I held her hand without speaking. This small unspoken gesture always let her know that she was in a judgement free zone, that she had my undivided attention, and that she could confide in me about anything. As she avoided my eye contact, I saw a huge tear run down her cheek. I reached in my back pack and handed her a tissue, "Take a deep breath and your time. Share whatever you desire." She wiped her tears, "Yes ma'am." My heart was beating so fast that even I had to take a breath as she continued. "My friend is in trouble and I don't know how to help her." I leaned towards her, "Don't tell me her name. Let's pretend your friend is you. Now imagine what Shannon would do?" She quickly replied, "It's not me mom!" She looked to the ground. When Shannon isn't being truthful, she always speaks fast and looks at the ground in a defensive manner, but this time was different. I reached for her hand, "Ok, let's just call her Sandra. Honey, how is Sandra in trouble?" She shook her head, "Well Sandra's step–dad has been calling her names like retarded and slow because she has ADHD like me. He beats her when her mom isn't home. He makes her cook and do chores way after her bedtime because she isn't old enough to work and bring home a paycheck. He also cheats on her mother, who's sick and

Sandra doesn't like how he plays with her and her other sister's. Sandra told me that she wants to run away and live with us because our family seems so happy. I told her no, looks are deceiving and that I'm not that happy either. I told her that she might want to run away to her uncle's house since her step dad told her he would beat the snot out of her." She turned to me, "He even hit Sandra's mom before. Did I tell Sandra the right thing to do? Because she's thinking about running away really soon." I instantly knew my Shannon was Sandra. As I cleared my throat, I held back my tears and screamed within. I sympathetically replied to my little princess, "Tell your friend Sandra she's very smart and that she isn't slow or retarded. You tell her that it's NOT her fault and to be sure to let her mother know how he beats and plays with her. Tell her not to forget how and where these things happened. Also, tell her to do the best she can to help her mom out anyway she can. Let her know that she's loved and very special and that her mom would really want to know how sad she is." I paused, "Ok Shannon?" Still with her eyes downward, she replied, "Yes ma'am." I reached for her hand once more, "I'll write all of this down so you won't forget to tell your friend, okay." As we sang a few songs together, I pulled her close and played in her long spiral coils. I was relieved in knowing that I wasn't crazy. Thank You Lord for the spirit of discernment!

April 2014

I stayed busy with therapy so that I could return to work with such progress that my doctors would rewrite their letters so that my job would rehire me with accommodations. I had been awarded medically retired Social Security and Pension; however, I was also willing to let Social Security go to achieve my seniority, pay, and benefits back. Meanwhile, I continued receiving data entry of Anthony's phone calls to Bethany, but my mother needed my help more than ever as time got closer to her Wedding Anniversary, so dealing with Anthony had to wait. As my mother received counseling for chronic depression, I sat silently receiving help for myself. The silent help didn't stop there. As I sat in on Shannon's sessions, I received a second dose of psychological help as Shannon's therapist conversed with her about our livelihood which apparently triggered frequent bed wetting, attitudes, her grades dropping, and so on. Not to mention, I seemed to be at the alter every Sunday praying and crying out to God for clarity and direction as to what to do in this situation. Later, Anthony had roses delivered to the house and a card which read: *You seem to like the roses from Shannon best, great progress! Your Husband A.* That weekend he took me shopping and purchased over $200.00 worth of under garments as a belated Valentines gift. He said they were for my "come-back" celebration whatever that meant. He seemed to have admired my hard work and efforts to go back to work and shockingly, on our way back home he smiled, "Tink, I wanna make all of our wrongs right. I want to wipe the slate clean and move forward." I looked at him in disbelief after he leaned over and kissed my cheek. Sadly, I didn't know how to respond to his oh so kind gesture. He looked over at me, "It's cool. I know it'll take time for you to open back up to me." I scoffed, "Why is it so hard for you to humble yourself, admit you're wrong, apologize from the heart, and even acknowledge why you're sorry in the first place? Shocked, he answered back, "Yeah you're right! My bad for all of it. Now let it go." I shook my head in disbelief, "Are you kidding me? Yeah, well my bad too Mr. Head of the household." After that, I didn't even open the gift that he gave me. That night he sautéed onions, bell peppers, mushrooms, and marinated only one 12 oz., T-bone steak while I prepared six thick pork chops with spinach, mashed potatoes, dinner rolls, strawberry short cake, and freshly cut strawberries. It took a while with my arm in a sling, but I managed through tolerable pain. I looked over at Anthony, "Why is there only one steak in the refrigerator!" He dropped his fork, "I'm the only one in this house working with a paycheck and I think I deserve a T-Bone steak for myself every once in a while, and I'll do it again woman!" Shannon immediately asked to be excused from the table in which we both said yes. As soon as Shannon was out of site, I shot back, "How dare you bring anything in this house that we your family can't partake of. That's the most selfish thing I've ever heard you say to date (I think). Shannon is a child and I didn't ask to leave my job." He replied sarcastically, "No you quit or you deliberately got fired!" I was heated, "False. I wouldn't have gotten awarded Social Security less than 30 days nor a lifetime pension if I had done either. It's not my fault that I inherited sickle cell anemia. You knew I had it and a preexisting condition before you married me. As a housewife, you never get paid as you would in the workforce, nor is there ever any time off. Oh, and understand this, when I was working full time, I managed this household and my family without lack, ever. Now that life has happened to me, I can give 100% to my family and home duties without being totally burnt out and exhausted. You don't have a clue or appreciation. You're being utterly unfair and unsupportive. I try to help by giving you $200.00 a month to help with bills and I guess that's not enough. Not to mention, I'm going to therapy three times a week and trying to get my physicians to reconsider rewriting a letter of recommendation to allow me to return to work. Why are you punishing me? Things in life change to adjust to. Have you forgotten our vows, your promise to God?" He replied in disgust, "First of all, I married a working woman. Those vows don't mean anything if they're one-sided." My blood pressure was so high my nose started bleeding. Shannon ran in the dining room and screamed, "Mama, daddy please stop it. If ya'll don't love each other just get a divorce so we can all be happy." Anthony, stood up and gave her a standing ovation. The next day there were three T-bone steaks apparently from his feelings of guilt; however, I didn't eat it. I chose to eat the left-over pork chops.

Exposed Evil

Anthony printed stunning 4th of July invitations for friends and family with our last year's family portrait of us smiling. He later asked me to mail out all of the invitations in which I (DID NOT). Instead I threw them in our outside dumpster. I signed a loan for us to have our porch extended, bought decorations, and kept the receipt to return everything so that Anthony would stop pressing me as to why I hadn't done so. We purchased $500.00 worth of food and beverages, a 200-pound hog to roast, plenty of games, party favors, and he even rented a karaoke machine with his said overtime money. I guess the garbage can must've spoke because he stormed in the kitchen and slapped a soggy invitation on the table, "You've sabotaged the entire party. Why?" I pulled out all of the proof that I had available in regards to he and Bethany, "You first Mr. Man of the house." Taken back, his demeanor changed, "I'm truly sorry. I won't call her anymore. Forgive me. You didn't deserve this. Tink, I never slept with her, but I did cheat by talking to her." I coughed up a laugh, "You're only sorry because you got caught. Besides, I decided not to send the invitations, so, I threw them in the garbage dumpster. I refuse to be fake and have a party like everything is alright." I took a deep breath and the pointing began, "You can't be serious with your ridiculous contract, your man cave, your mean spirited ways, your nasty comments, your cheating, your invoice to extra receipts you thought you got rid of inside your garbage can, you accusing me of quitting my job, your charging me out of spite and buying a T-bone steak for yourself. You must be crazy. Shannon is afraid of you, you don't support her, and not to mention, you lied about your anger management because it's down-right mean." He got down on his knees with tears in his eyes begging, but I walked off like a Boss. Although I was relieved that his lies were now exposed, the question still remained, what now? He emailed, texted, called, and visited everyone he invited for the sake of not losing so much money and efforts to pull off a great family outing. He looked at me, "We need a turn-around with fun and laughter, besides, I have a surprise for you. I promise to make it right." Once again, I forgave him, but my heart was damaged. Led by my emotions, my social media post read:

Without communication, there is NO relationship. Without respect there is NO love. There is NO love without trust. Where there is NO trust, there is NO reason to continue. One day, you're going to wake up and notice that you should have tried. I was "Worth" the fight. (In ALL Caps) He heard about the post and the many comments like, what's going on Katie? Needless to say, he asked me to delete it because it was causing people on his job and at his church to question if our marriage was in trouble. Anthony thought it was sending subliminal messages and by the time I took the post down, enough people had read it to know it was a cry for help. I truly didn't mean to expose what was going on behind closed doors by indirectly putting our business out into the world for people to gossip about. I once read perception is everything, but I was simply venting for myself only. The people in our rather large circle already knew we were unhappy and that our marriage was in trouble, but they didn't know how much trouble. My mom, Shannon, and I later went to a small town called Slocomb, where my mom would purchase or pick fresh vegetables. She knew of a Cuban woman who prepared jerk chicken and goat there for us to purchase for the festives. She was heavy-set olive-skinned woman with a long braid down her back. Shortly after we arrived, she came out of her smokehouse with well-seasoned aromas of sausage links, salted bacon, ham, chicken, lamb, veal, and yes goat. She walked over and smiled, "Come my child, let mama Joesiphena (Meaning Feeler of Your Heart) talk with you". She first took my mom's hand and looked her deeply in the eyes, "No more sad days, no more tears over your loss. Move forward!" I sat in awe as my mom grabbed her hand, "Thank you mama Joe, I feel my joy coming." I was shaking when she reached out her chubby hand for mine. The great thing for me is that we never made eye contact. She drew me slowly to her ample bosom as if she had wings to usher me in. I was getting ready to speak and she placed a finger to her lips, "Shhhhh. Let me hear your heart speak." I took a deep breath, closed my eyes, and wrapped my arms around her thick waist. Mama Joe continued, "Get ready and be strong, most importantly Progerlar, in her first language (Meaning Protect Her)." She released me as she pointed to Shannon standing like a deer in headlights. Mama Joe clapped her hands loudly, "Speak your truth child, don't be afraid. You've done nothing wrong." I ran to her and held her as she sobbed uncontrollably, "Shannon please help me, help you. Please tell me what's wrong. I want to help you baby." Mama Joe interjected, "Not here babies. There are too many ears. Take your goat and take courage on your journey to come." Instantly I recalled the warnings of Dr. Sees, Shannon's

friend in trouble, other warnings, my nightmares, and now
Mama Joe.

Renewing Vows

Before preparing for our 4th of July festive, Anthony asked
me to take out a $5000.00 loan to build a beautiful screened
in porch and roof with electricity and two ceiling fans. Out
of the $1,000.00 left over, Anthony didn't seem to be happy
until it was all gone. "Hey Tink, I need $100.00 for fireworks,
$75.00 for a portable shower to put near the pool, $100.00 for
a portable potty to keep traffic out of the house, $200.00 for
more beer, wine, liquor, ice, and juice." I wondered to
myself, *who is he trying to impress?* Just say, time passed by
quickly because the day of the party was finally here. Many
and of Anthony's family and children stayed in local hotels
while my family stayed with Marie being that her house was
large enough to comfortably house eight family members
from GA and FL. Normally, I would have been patriotic but
instead I wore a black swimsuit covering as if I were in
mourning and I was. I thought to myself, *I wonder if Anthony*
has confided in any of his siblings outside of his oldest sister
who said they'd be coming to the merged family celebration
about our now issues. You see, I mainly told God about all
our problems because I was always told to keep folks and
family out of our marriage. In spite of it all, I had to regroup

118

because I wanted Anthony's moms first visit to our home to be a nice one. It was absolutely nice to see all who had come from both near and far to celebrate with us. Besides, we had some great cooks on both sides of the family who all seemed to get along. I sat by smiling as Anthony's mom enjoyed the smoked goat Mama Joe had cooked that she requested to have when she arrived to the party. I loved her in spite of her immobility, alcoholism, and her battle with cancer. Just say we were pleasantly surprised that she was miraculously in remission! God is truly a divine healer, that I do know. My brother sat in the corner observing as he smoked his cigar and sipped his brown liquor. He would usually be the one on the grill setting up making sure everyone was comfortable. Although he wasn't a faker, something was a little off and I couldn't put my finger on it. Anthony offered a quick prayer and word of thanks to all whom had traveled near and far. "Hey ya'll. Be sure to eat, drink in moderation, go around, and introduce yourself." He looked my way as if he were waiting for me to say something. So, I lifted my champagne glass and toasted to Independence. Before I could take a sip, Anthony smiled, "Hold up Tink! Remember I said I had a surprise? Well, close your eyes and hold out your left hand." I felt something feathery on my head, then something cold on my ring finger. When they took the blindfold off, Anthony was down on one knee with a bouquet of tulips. I had removed my wedding ring months ago and apparently; he hadn't noticed it. Out of the corner of my eye, I saw my brother get up and leave. Anthony noticed too, but he cleared his throat and continued, "Baby will you do me the honor of renewing our vows in front of God and these witnesses?" In shock, I didn't even look down at my ring. Just say, I immediately felt like I was on some game show with all eyes on me waiting for me to give the correct answer. I took a deep breath, "Anthony, the gesture is very nice, but so unnecessary. We're already married. Let's renew our vows when we've been married at least ten to twenty years." I paused and looked at him, "Okay." Someone in the background shouted, "Get up off your knee Pops! You aint gotta beg her!" He looked back, "Whoever said that, shut up. I put this woman through hell and back. She's suffered five major surgeries, sickle cell, and now she's trying to make a come-back for her job. I want and need for her to come back to me." (Crickets) He continued, "Tink, I'm sorry. My hidden agenda was to impress everyone and make them think we were happy and had everything together, but I also wanted you to feel like my wife and not a trophy. Please accept this ring and consider our vows we promised before God." Now ain't that the pot calling the kettle black. *Thank you, Jesus, for fixing this one.* I didn't have to embarrass him any further, so I gave him a hug and acknowledged that piece of ice on my finger. He smiled to cover the shame, "We'll table this until we discuss matters in private, but for now let's have fun." It was gonna take more than an expensive piece of jewelry that he couldn't afford to make up for the way he had previously treated me and my daughter. We prayed, ate, danced, and took photos. After the awkward proposal to renew our vows, I thought everyone was at ease, but my cousin (Prophetess Taylor) had an issue with Anthony riding the kids under the water on his back and ignoring my words for him to not do so for obvious reasons so they removed their preteen daughter Renee' from the pool. Not only did they remove her from the pool, they also got her dressed and left before the family photos could be taken. I thought I'd take a mental note as to why the urgency to remove their child so quickly. Being that she was a prophet, I could now see why. Anthony walked over to me, "Tink, I need the remaining money to cover cost of alcohol, gas, hotel cost for my sisters and brothers, nieces and nephews, and the grandkids." I thought to myself, *Really! I would have liked to have known before-hand.* In my opinion, everyone had a whole year to prepare and save their own money, especially after he contacted them personally when I threw the invitations away. I had no problem helping family financially because I had to ask for help with our wedding, but an entire family of twenty-three all at one time was too much.

Although he promised they would pay us back in full, it was the principle of the matter. We couldn't afford for this to bite us after the party was over. As the night went on, we experienced fireworks in more ways than one. I continued to contribute my willingness to try to move forward even in knowing we had a lot of work ahead of us in our marriage. For now, I needed and wanted to be alert with this many people in and out of our house, but Anthony assumed that I was tipsy. The funny thing is that I didn't even have one drop of alcohol. The fact that there were so many people there that suffered from alcoholism made me really uncomfortable. My sisters noticed how tired I was and rounded the men up to clean the tables, pool, and the yard while the women took care of the entire house and food. I had to be at church at eight the next morning to sing off of five hours of sleep. I was exhausted. Anthony woke up early that morning and cooked a grand breakfast. How he had the energy to do so, I'll never know. From the apparent description that Anthony gave his family of me, they were shocked to learn that I was this down to earth country woman. As for my family and friends, the one thing they knew about me was that I didn't do fake. My sister n law looked at me, "I see that it's very difficult for you to fit in." Exhausted, I simply responded, "I don't know what Anthony has told ya'll about me, but I know my place and I'm just Kay.

I'm not in competition with anyone." Anthony explained, "I may have given them the wrong impression of you when they first met you." I looked at Anthony, "This is my house and if I can't be myself without make-up, jeans, and a T-shirt, then that's too bad. I refuse to be phony or fake. Before everyone departed, I gave a few expensive items away that my oldest step-daughter and sister in laws admired as well as my very last $60.00 for them to have enough gas money to make it home. It seemed to me that what we had done just wasn't enough. We waved good bye and Shannon and I went to bed early knowing that Shannon had school the next morning. Anthony tinkered around in our office and moved back in his cave after resetting it from where his mother slept.

Be Careful What You Ask For

Every morning for three weeks straight, I would wake up early with deep feelings of acrimony overtaking me because my spirit was vexed. I immediately fell on my knees and asked God to reveal that which had my muscles tense in knots and my heartbeat dancing to the tunes of frustration. "Lord prepare me for what lies ahead and please give me the wisdom to act appropriately." I needed and wanted God to reveal whatever was going on to me no matter how painful, ugly, or disturbing it was. I felt strong enough to face this giant just as David did against Goliath. (Side Note) Be careful what you ask for! I had finally dozed back off to sleep after another one of my nightmares, forcing me to a strong urgency to pray when I heard trickling sounds of water from the shower at about 4:30 a.m., which made me have to pee. I got up and went into our master bathroom and found our bathroom door locked with Anthony inside, but the shower was fogging up the entire bathroom. I staggered to Shannon's bathroom and sat on the toilet in the dusk dark. I held my face in my hands, "Lord, thank you for another day, but Lord I don't like being unhappy anymore." When I lifted my head and opened my eyes BOOM I saw a red and green light flickering. After I flushed the toilet and washed my hands, I turned the light on and the colors vanished! I thought *hmmmm, how odd*. So, I turned the light off and the lights reappeared. I sat on the toilet and realized Shannon's alarm clock was on; however, her alarm clock light was light blue. Being that I am a very meticulous person with OCD, my eyes can be very analytical. As I continued to investigate this light, I noticed that the zebra printed towel trimmed in hot pink was shifted. I sat on the toilet once more and I flipped the towel over to see what was making it look crooked. "What the hell?" I gasped for air with my hands over my mouth, jumped up, and put cold water on my face followed by vomiting and diarrhea. My heart pumped so fast that my nose began to bleed. I yelled, "My God, my God! What evil is this?" I flushed the toilet once more, wiped my nose and face with a cold wet towel, and then, the tears flowed. I couldn't believe my eyes. There was a domino size camera ducked taped through a hole behind my babies' towel with red and green lights flickering apparently recording her. This was the most heinous sick act I've ever encountered. I took a deep breath and charged into our bathroom for answers from him, It, Legion, Anthony whoever this monster was. As I held up the camera still attached to the towel, I was livid, "What in the hell is going on?" Startled, he pulled back the shower curtain, "I can explain, let me get the soap suds rinsed off of my face first." I began slapping him as hard as I could in the face and even harder against his head. He got out of the shower and reached for his towel as he covered his head with his hands. He yelled, "Stop it!" I was livid, "You SOB, you better have a good explanation for this evil you've committed." He sat at the edge of our garden tub shaking while drying off refusing any eye contact. I jerked his chin up towards me, "Talk dammit." He looked away, "I was only trying to find out what was taking her so long in the bathroom." All I could do was shake my head, "Whatever! For only you to see the video." He tried to explain once more, "This explains why she keeps missing the bus. It was stupid of me to get the camera without telling you, but I didn't mean any harm. Only you would've viewed the footage. I'm sorry it's not what it looks like." I snapped, "Exactly what does it look like (at the top of my voice). At what point was I to be the only one to view this footage without you seeing what was on the recording first?" More lies rolled from his tongue, "I know this makes me look like a creepy 'Peeping-Tom' I guess." I shot back, "No guessing. This is a criminal act of a Pedophile. Do you know what this means? Are you sexually attracted to (MY) child or other children her age?" Taken back, he replied, "God No...Woman." I was over it, "Don't put God into this now, you twisted demon. Put your robe on and show me what you've recorded on this camera from your computer." As we rushed to our office, I pushed him down into the chair as I held one hand inside my pajama pants to make him think I had a gun. He spoke nervously, "Please don't do anything crazy." My eyes penetrated his soul, "Oh, you're gonna see crazy if my child is on this computer." He hooked the camera to the computer and pressed play. It showed my face looking downward with tears in my eyes mouthing, "What the hell is this at 5:02 a.m." He looked up, "That's all I promise. I just put it in there for the first time ever." I insisted that he press rewind, but there was nothing. Livid, I screamed, "GIVE IT TO ME NOW SOB!" He fell on his knees, "Why? What are you going to do with it? I know now I should've come to you first." In awe, I looked at him, "Do you think I would've ever consented to this stupidity? My daughter had already explained to myself and her therapist as to why she was always late. I knew she was folding up a towel to take a nap on her bathroom floor while she covered up with her robe to stay warm. Had you asked you would've known that sometimes she would be on her phone not paying attention to time causing her to be late which I took the phone away from her. You would've known that she was taking too much time primping with her hair, as girls do, not being mindful of time passing by. I was on top of the situation, but apparently you decided to take pedophilic actions into your own inexcusable hands. Bring yourself into her bathroom." As we walked into the bathroom, I pointed, "Do you see exactly where your camera was pointing? It's where she does her business on the toilet. When she gets out of the shower, that means that you can see that too. So, that means you have visual access to seeing her nude body, not to mention, you could see her getting dressed. Now for the last time Give Me the Camera!" His hands were noticeably fidgeting as he handed it over. "Are you deleting something?" Nervously her replied, "No! I'm just turning it off." Shannon woke up and yelled, "What now? This is why I hate coming home. Ya'll are always arguing." My heart sank to hear this from her. "Why are ya'll in my bathroom? I'm not sleeping, eating, or on my phone in there anymore." I looked over at her, "Your daddy decided to put a video camera in your bathroom behind this towel with a hole in it and recorded YOU!" He attempted to cover up his wrong doings, "No Tink, you didn't need to tell her." I looked at him in awe, "Why not? It's all about her isn't it? She has a right to know. Her privacy and her innocence have been violated." I had to restrain myself from cursing around her, especially hard-core F-bomb words. Her eyes filled with tears as her bottom lip trembled, "D-a-d-d-y is this true? Did you see me naked?" "No, baby-girl, even your mom saw that I didn't." Confused, she answered back, "Well were you going to see me naked when you pressed play on the camera?" His eyes shifted from me to her, "No again, WE just wanted to see why you kept missing the bus." I was so angry, I kicked him in the knee aiming for his balls, "We, don't you ever use (We), this was all you and you alone. Own up to your own crap." As she left hysterically crying, I went to console her. "Mom I want to get out of here and go to school. I can't deal with this." She brushed her teeth and washed her face in our bathroom with me in there with her while Anthony went inside of his man cave sniffing and begging for forgiveness. As I watched Shannon get on the bus with her puffy red eyes, I drove off with my purse and camera in my pajamas. I went to Burger King down the street because I felt sick again. I started hyperventilating and grabbed a plastic bag that was in the car to breathe inside of it slowly and calmly. I tried to call my voice of reason; my oldest sister Leslie, but I'm sure at that hour she was battling traffic to work. Then, I called my middle sister Marie, the calm/no panic spirited one. She answered, "What's up Chica?" I struggled to get the words out, "I need you now, it's an emergency." She asked concerned, "Is this a sickle cell crisis hun?" I wiped my eyes, "No, I'm sitting in my car in my pajamas." (Silence) She asked, "Are you able to meet me behind Walmart?" In minutes she and Candy arrived together. Candy started to jump out of the car and hug me, but I placed my hand up to stop her. Marie asked, "Did Anthony hit you?" As she walked towards me, I held up my hand once more, "No, it'll only make me cry uncontrollably. I need to be able to tell you without losing my mind." Candy looked at me with concern, "Ok, from the top, we can be late for work. Take your time." I was talking so fast before I started crying. Marie handed me some Kleenex. I didn't miss a beat! When I finished, they both looked at me with wide eyes and their mouths opened wide. "Oh, hell naw!" Candy used every curse word known to man that I restrained myself from just to get out the rage. Just say, she said everything I wanted to say. Marie asked, "Katie is he dead?" I shook my head, "Not yet." I showed my sisters the camera, but Candy being the very technical savvy one looked at me, "Give me

129

the sim card Kay! It's a small microchip that you need to record with. It goes inside of the camera." I reached for it, "This is all he gave me." Marie shook her head, "He's hiding something!" I took a deep breath, "When I saw the recording, it was a reflection of me on his computer." You could see the anger in Candy's eyes as she spoke, "No ma'am you only saw what he wanted you to see! I promise you; he's deleting everything right now. You need to get that hard drive immediately, like right now. Where is Shannon?" I paused for a second, "She went to school a mess." My sisters shook their heads as I continued, "I called the police and wrote a statement, while yet in my pajamas. Without any evidence, I couldn't press charges nor could they issue a warrant to search the house or remove his hard drive. They said that I could file for a restraining order to protect Shannon, so I did!" After doing so, I got a shower and ate, then I went to Shannon's school to give the counselor a copy of the of the restraining order. After I left, my sisters and I waited for Anthony's car to be gone, hopefully to work, so we could get some clothes. Marie looked at me, "You could stay with me and our mom until we figure out what to do." I packed enough clothes, shoes, food, and my entire filing cabinet that would hold us for a few months being that I wasn't sure if I was going back. Within three days, I made an appointment to speak with an attorney. Anthony blew up my phone all night long, but I didn't answer! He messaged me reminding me that we had an appointment at the house with the mortgage agent to sign a lower percentage rate towards our principle and mortgage cost. I replied back, *our house is no longer a home because of the sick choices you made. I'll sign the documents, but it doesn't mean that I'm coming back to that house. One thing I'm not, is stupid!* I knew that my name, money, blood, sweat, and tears were invested and I wasn't just going to turn it over that easy, no matter the outcome. I packed my 380 automatic with one of my dad's favorite hunting jackets before arriving to this strange place I once called home. The real estate agent pointed to certain lines for Anthony to sign and date. She seemed nervous as she looked into my blood shot red eyes and addressed me slowly, "Hiiiii." Without looking at either of them, I asked, "Where do I sign ma'am?" She attempted to break the tension that could clearly cut clean through air, "It looks like stormy weather is on its way." I shot back, "Correction ma'am, the storm is already here!" Reluctantly, her eyes grew wide, "Okayyyyyy! Just two more signatures Mrs. Rappt and we're done." The pen shook in my hand as anger took over me because I was so hurt and confused. As I walked her to the door, Anthony jumped up behind me, "Please don't go until you've heard what I need to say. I'm sorry and I'll never spy on Shannon again. Tink, I promise, my intentions were pure. I love you both. Please don't divorce me. Bring my baby girl back." He didn't stop there, "I promise that I won't horse play with Shannon anymore. I'll do whatever you ask of me for us to stay together. Besides, Shannon isn't my type!" My mouth almost hit the floor, "What the hell! What teenager is?" He giggled, "No! Wait, obviously that came out wrong. I meant Shannon is a child and I desire a woman." Pissed off and disgusted, I went off, "Seriously, any woman will do, not me your wife?" He tried to fix it again, "I can't explain it. I promise, I only desire you." He held up his hands, "I'll find out medically why I lost my sex drive!" I scoffed, "Is there anything else you need to tell me? More camera's... What happened to the SIM card? What are you hiding in your man cave? Have you ever slept with a minor? Are you still calling your ex or sleeping with anyone?" He took a deep breath, "No to all of your questions, except I destroyed the SIM card because I didn't know what you were planning on doing with it. If you had went to the police, they could've and would've arrested me, then we would have lost our home. In that order!" He proceeded, "I did sleep with my step-daughter's best friend (Sweetie) when she was 17 and I was in my early thirties. It only happened once and she consented, so it wasn't rape!" If looks could kill, he'd be dead. "Anthony, you're dead wrong for that. She was a minor and you were a grown ass man. You make me sick!" He rubbed

132

his chin, "I love you Tink, please take as much time as you need. I'll do whatever it takes to save our marriage." I looked at him with tears in my eyes, "What's love got to do with this?" I thought to myself, *The mind of a pedophile feeds on grooming and manipulation. It's almost like a hunger that can never truly be fed. How did this get past me?* I wondered if this too was concealed under a microscope of disguise, now being revealed by faith? Shannon was eager to forgive and said, "Mamma, yeah he was stupid, but I'm fine, nothing happened. Can we go back home, I'm sure he's learned his lesson. Just make him sign a contract like you did for me to keep my room and bathroom clean and if he doesn't keep his word, then, they'll be serious consequences just as there was for me if I didn't keep my end of the bargain." She shrugged her shoulders, "He just won't be grounded. He'll be divorced." My siblings and mother said, "You're gonna have to live with whatever decision you make, but whatever you do above all things, protect Shannon." Although, they lost respect for Anthony, but it hurt that they lost respect for me. Needless to say, I made the decision to go back with the understanding that he would sign, date and notarize a binding contract stating that if he didn't comply to all that was within it, it would be grounds for divorce. Finally, after being separated for thirty-three days, we began marriage counseling both individually and collectively. I had come to the conclusion that I didn't want to believe my husband had a "thing" for my daughter or that he wanted her in any sexual way. It wasn't the typical I'm sorry that he was caught type of thing, it truly seemed real this time. Besides, forgiveness was key. So, I decided to fight for my marriage. We never had spiritual counseling, because Anthony was too embarrassed for either one of our pastors to know what he had done. During marriage counseling, he showed an effort to make our marriage work by owning up to his mistakes, acknowledging that he was willing to change, and agreeing to sign the contract. If God could forgive me for my potty mouth and the mean things I had secretly done to my husband when I found out he was talking to his ex, then God could forgive him and save our marriage! It hurt really bad that my sister, Marie and a few friends thought I went back because of the house, income and other perks, such as a retired military wife. I just wish they would've understood that my reason for going back was to fight for my marriage.

My Contract:

The contract went a little like this, *I Anthony Rappt, agree to never lie about anything again. I will refrain from ALL camera usage within the home around Shannon or any minors, I will no longer horse play with Shannon, and I will refrain from all negative comments such as, retard to make Shannon feel bad... I will go to ALL appointments for professional anger management where documentation will be provided as proof. I will no longer charge my wife monthly income out of spite because she is unable to work at this time. I will be more involved with Shannon's IEP courses and doctor's appointments. I will take every aspect of my wife's sickle cell seriously with the understanding that my wife becomes fatigued at times, I will no longer steal my wife's medication, and I will be sure to take my wife to the ER quickly without any negative comments to be treated. I will try to resolve issues quickly being sure not let the sun go down on my anger and make sure that I take the time to communicate with my wife to resolve issues. I will be mindful to control my volume and tone of voice, especially when I'm angry. I acknowledge that my wife gives me permission to verbally correct Shannon and use other disciplinary actions; however, I do not have any permission to lay a hand on her daughter again... I will try to love my wife as Christ loves the church. I will not make my wife regret coming back to me. I understand and agree that if I fail to abide by this agreement, it will be as if I used a gun, pulled the trigger, and killed this family.*

Signed Kay,

Let's Rebuild

I had graduated from therapy with limited mobility in the midst of rebuilding our family, marriage, and my strength. Overtime, I gained even more mobility and I was so grateful to God for that, not to mention, Anthony was actually putting in some effort to abide by our contract. I was finally awarded social security and pension income that would ease some of our financial strain. It seemed as though everything was going great, that is until Anthony began receiving writeups for threatening co-workers and falling asleep at his desk during work. Not to mention, he was constantly arguing with his first shift supervisor over parking spaces assigned to those in lead positions. With an attempt to finally get back to work, I provided my job with all documentation and two letters from my physicians approving me to return to work with a limited work load to avoid any further injury to my shoulder. Even in providing all of the necessary documents, I felt as though they were giving me the run around by stalling to make a decision. A few weeks later, Shannon decided to make an intimate Thanksgiving dinner with my supervision and although the colorful garnish was appealing to the eye and the dinner was absolutely delicious, my heart still hurt in knowing that no one invited us to the family Thanksgiving dinner. We felt like outcasts and it just seemed that no one wanted to deal with us anymore. I guess them knowing so much of what was going on in our marriage caused them to feel as though we would only put a damper on the family functions. Christmas was the same so we decided to make the best of it. As a family we enjoyed each other as we put up our Christmas decorations. After a long day and night, we prepared for bed and to my surprise, Anthony used his sleep apnea machine; however, during our private time, it disturbed me as I remembered the flashing lights from the camera. There were great moments as we worked to rebuild our family and marriage like, Shannon's behavior seemed to improve at school and home, but her relationship with Anthony was very strange. Although she accepted Anthony's apology, she never looked at him the same again. They seemed to dodged each other and that caused me to become very paranoid. That being said, it was crucial for me to make sure that Shannon was cautious of what she wore around him. I searched the house high and low during my daily cleaning to assure that there were no hidden cameras and Shannon did the same. She made sure to cover any space that a camera could be hidden with small strips of duct tape, especially in the bathroom. A few days later, I took Shannon Christmas shopping and gave her $50.00 to spend as she desired. She wanted an upgrade on her phone but I refused; however, Anthony purchased it against my will with his bonus check. I guess he assumed that this kind gesture would take away the permanent damage he had done, but giving Shannon his entire bonus check couldn't make that go away. Normally, I would have completed shopping by October for everyone but my income was extremely limited and I couldn't be as generous as before. On Christmas Day, we exchanged gifts as I baked my signature Red Velvet cake, watched Christmas movies, and drank egg nog. I couldn't just ignore my family, so I sent out Christmas and New Year Eve cards to everyone, but no one replied. Shannon knew that her grandmother was dying of cancer and seeing her ASAP was necessary, so Anthony booked a hotel for us to visit her. We picked up my mom and left on December 30th and planned to return on January 3rd. We took my mother because she and Anthony's mom were good friends. Besides, December was daddy's birthday and January was their Wedding Anniversary and we wanted her to celebrate with us. I just didn't want her to be sad, alone, and depressed. We had previously drawn names during our 4th of July party and in spite of not being invited to the holiday dinners, we chose to give Anthony's side of the family their gifts while we were there. We celebrated during the New Year's Eve card game party at Anthony's youngest sister's house and boy was

Shannon excited to see her cousins. Once were settled in our rooms, we got dressed, and walked out with gifts in our hands, along with a huge poinsettia for my mother-in-law. You would have thought that Anthony was done trying to showcase me as his trophy wife, but he wasn't. He asked me to wear a knee length black sequenced cocktail dress he purchased me three years before in spite of my apparent weight gain; therefore, causing me to walk in with all eyes on me in this dress that now fit like a glove. Although, Nicole (Anthony's Sister) had a nice size house that was beautifully decorated, it was very crowded. The children had the back playroom and the adults remained in the kitchen den (Poolroom) and living room, while others stood on the balcony firing fireworks. Male and female waiters arrived with beautifully assembled hors d'oeuvres, a tasty seafood feast, champagne, and a variety of delightful desserts, but I couldn't help but to notice that the waiters were inappropriately dressed. Just say they looked like exotic dancers. I was so embarrassed that I immediately sent Shannon in the back room and sat with my mother in the den and began playing spades. I kissed mother Rappt on her cheek and to my surprise, I smelled alcohol on her breath. As I gave her the Poinsettia, she looked at me, "Where's my red velvet cake daughter?" I smiled, "Mother, I wanted to bake you one but I didn't have time. Besides, it would've been better to make a fresh one instead of risking it cracking during the travel." She gave me that look, "Well shugga, there's no time like the present. The kitchen is all yours." I smiled, "Yes ma'am." I passed right by that kitchen and went straight to the bar for a much needed stiff drink. I looked at the bar tender and dug deep, "I'll have a Shirley Temple." Shocked, he replied, "Really"? I scoffed, "I need to keep a clear head while making my mothers-in-law her favorite dessert." I got my drink and walked into the kitchen where Anthony helped me with my apron and all the ingredients. He placed his hand on my back, "I would have rescued you if I were there." He paused, "Look, I'm sorry, I know you didn't come here to cook, but no one has ever told my mom no." I shook my head, "I guess not, but you need to tell her to put that whiskey down. He smirked, "Somebody must've slipped her some liquor." He took a sip of his drink, "I'll check on you in a bit. I'm about to shoot some fireworks with Simon." I despised Simon and I truly lost respect for him when he would brag about his extra marital affairs and his love pads in Alabama and Georgia to my husband. Not to mention, he was a womanizer who constantly left his family behind to commute to his job that was four hours away. Simon – Mo = SIN Boom, there you have it. I felt it very disrespectful as to how he treated and cheated on his wife, and how he took advantage of the fact that he knew as long as he gave her 80% of his check and didn't give her any STD's, she would be okay with it. I lost total respect for her and kept an obvious distance because I didn't want that type of influence in my life. I walked into Anthony's sister's extravagant top chef kitchen and began whipping up the ingredients for my signature Red Velvet cake. I could see Anthony and Simon puffing their cigars, toasting with liquor in their glasses from the window as I chopped a few pecans for the frosting. Before I knew it, my radar sensory hearing was triggered by inappropriate conversation because the slide door was open, but I kept my head down quietly, chopping away at the pecans. As their backs were turned, the inappropriate conversation continued and before I knew it, Anthony's ex Bethany's name was mentioned, followed with a heated argument that led to loud voices, cursing, and Anthony slamming the door so hard that I thought it cracked. Shortly thereafter, Anthony walked over to me and offered me at least four glasses of wine, "Do you want to have your way with me by getting me drunk?" As I poured each glass down the drain, he frowned, "So what all did you hear?" I frowned back, "Enough!" When count down came, I hugged Shannon and started dancing to the Electric Slide with the kids. Our moms were two shakes in the wind. Anthony and Simon were on the patio shooting their guns and fireworks. If you ask me, it was very dangerous mix with alcohol. I yelled, "Anthony, do you want some crab legs?" He nodded and screamed, "Happy New Year!" With no embrace, no kiss, no dancing, no nothing, I walked into the dining room, "That's fine with me." His very drunk buddy Simon came into the dining room and deliberately patted my behind followed up with a slick comment, "I should've skinned you a long time ago." I grabbed the entire pot of hot grits and splashed them on him, then busted him in the head with the pot until his head started gushing with blood. I fell to my knees in disbelief and started crying. Shannon and her cousin were playing hide and seek under the nearby large table that sat ten people when they ran over and jumped on top of Simon biting, kicking, and slapping him. Shannon kicked him again, "You dirty dog. You have no business touching my mom's butt." As he lay there screaming for help, Anthony staggered into the dining room and screamed, "Meagan, Shannon, get off of him. What's going on?" Anthony's nieces reached down, helped me up, and looked up at Simon in disgust. Everyone rushed into the dining room to see what the commotion was about. Confused, Anthony looked down at me, "Tink what happened?" As he reached down to help me off of the floor, I whispered, "Simon grabbed my behind and said he should have skinned me a long time ago. So, I poured the hot grits for the fried catfish on him. Shannon and Meagan saw and heard everything as they played under the table." Simon was washing his face at the sink, yelling, "She's lying man. I only gave her a love pat to congratulate her on the cake. Those little heifers got it all wrong." Shannon was livid as tears flowed down her face, "You're lying!" Anthony put his gun to Simon's head, "Tell me the truth." Simon laughed, "Man neither one of us knows what the truth is because we're both liars. We're one of the same. We both love our wives but we love our side chics too!" Everyone gasped as he continued, except for me. "Ain't that right T-Bone? In our military days, remember how you got your nickname. You were notorious for boning young chics." Anthony shouted, "Man shut the hell up. You're drunk. Did you touch my wife? I'm about to blow your freakin brains out right now." Anthony's mother walked in, "Son put your gun down. He's drunk." I guess Anthony didn't think before he spoke because his next words made him look guilty. Anthony yelled, "A drunk always tell the truth ain't that right, mama?" She slapped his mouth bloody, "I might be a drunk, but as your dying momma, you will respect me. You don't deserve your wife and that ain't no alcohol talking either." A fun family party turned into a nightmare. Anthony put his gun down, Simon, get your sorry behind up and tell my wife you're sorry." I pushed Anthony away, "Where's your apology to me?" I grabbed my mother and Shannon, then looked over at

Anthony's favorite nieces Michelle, "Please take us to our hotel." The sad part is, this jerk just let us leave. On our way there his niece looked at me as she drove, "Aunty I am so sorry. Men can be so stupid. Uncle Anthony was wrong to let Mr. Simon off the hook like that. He should've beat him to a pulp and it should have been him leaving with ya'll, not me." She looked back at Shannon, "Do me a favor little cuz and take care of yourself and your mom. Everything ain't what it seems." (another warning) Shannon replied, "What do you mean Mickey?" Michelle began singing an old hymn with my mom and looked back at Shannon, "In the end, you'll understand." I looked at Michelle and smiled, "Thank you. Be careful on your way back to the house." When we got to the hotel, we packed our suitcases in record time and I made reservations for another hotel across town. The next day, I rented a car and sang thank God it's Friday on our way back to Alabama without my spouse. My mom apologized for her drinking and for everything that had happened even though she didn't have a part in it. Very emotional about the situation, my mother reached for my hand, "I don't want to be around those bunches of mixed nuts anymore." She added, "What are you gonna do now that your back home?" I answered, "Mommy dearest it doesn't feel like home and I don't know." At that moment I had to quickly decide to "Fight or Flight" and I decided the latter. Just say, Anthony didn't come home until the 5th. He was calm until he saw that I had completely transformed his man cave back into our African theme guest bedroom, just as every bedroom was. He got in my face, "Change it back now, you left me!" Shannon stayed overnight with a friend I trusted until the next day. Thank God for small blessings. I had a few days to battle this spiritual warfare in prayer. I took him by the hand and I said, "Pray with me, don't fight with me. I'm not the enemy you need to be fighting against." I added, "Satan I see you for who you are and what you're trying to do. You're a liar. I know you come to kill, steal, and destroy. You are the author of confusion. If you get the head of this household, the entire family falls. I come to serve you notice. We serve a God who we stood before and witnesses that we vowed to love each other for sickness or health, for richer or poorer, through good times and bad, forsaken all others. We also promised to honor and cherish each other and support one another. You said you will provide for and protect us. We said we will be faithful to each other. We promised to be an example for Shannon. You promised to love me as Christ loves the church, Lord Jesus help us to keep our words and to act upon them with realness, as we activate our faith. Dear Jesus help us to speak those things that are not as thou they were. Forgive us for our sins. You said you will make this for our good and that no weapon formed against us shall not prosper. Satan, I speak with authority that I bind you back to the pits of hell and all of your assignments are cancelled in the name of Jesus and it is so amen. We lifted our teary eyes, "Anthony, are you in agreement with me? He quietly responded, "I really don't deserve you like my mama said." I stood firm on my words, "Well, we really don't deserve God's grace and mercy, but I know He's not lacking in His promises or multiple chances.

The Unfathomable

Monday, February 2, 2015 was now here and it was time to go before an administration panel of ten about my job where one of the panel members so happened to be member of my church named Johnnie. Unique name for a woman, but I thought she was kind and beautiful. I just wished she knew it. She was a milk chocolate, full figured, and very intelligent woman with thick, beautiful curly locs. Locs that many would die for. During each visit, I would always leave a sincere encouraging word for her. Not because she documented all of my prescribed control substances, but because she was my sister in Christ. I thank God that she was there because 10 minutes into the meeting, I would've been acting out of character with fury once I realized what the meeting was about. As for Mr. James Crater my Hispanic union representative who knew my husband from being in the military; he didn't represent me well at all. He had previously reviewed my files and informed me of what to expect over the phone for the briefing with absolutely no concern about my medical documentation or my authorized letters from my physicians that clearly stated that I could return to work with accommodations and could work any shift available. One of the panelists leaned forward and badgered me, "Ms. Kay, please explain why you didn't return to work upon the doctors first approval?" I shook my head, "In my defense, Ms. Lori with Human Resource informed me that I wouldn't be considered until I provided another letter from my doctor and possibly a third letter in my case in which I hand delivered the second letter as soon as it was available for pick up. I followed a direct order." I took a deep breath, I was later informed that you all never received the fax from Dr. Bonce', my third specialist surgeon." I scanned the room, "May I ask why she isn't here?" Please have someone to check your sign in/out sheet, view your surveillance cameras, and I will not object to a lie detector test right here, right now! My livelihood has been jeopardized here. Doesn't it mean anything to you that I am a certified worker that has never failed an alcohol or drug test with no write ups or complaints. I have never violated any rule and I have always followed your guidelines? Yes, I have a preexisting condition, but there are sex offenders, convicted felons, and people with other conditions who have violated business policies and now you're telling me I'm going to be terminated over an illness I have no control over." Mr. Crater interjected, "Excuse me ma'am Mrs. Rappt, you cannot say—" A soft spoken gentleman interrupted him, "Ms. Lori had an emergency and H.R doesn't have cameras or lie detectors. We only have sign in/out sheets, but you are welcome to view your records to see if there was an oversight. We can only discuss the documents we have for us and we can only discuss your situation, not others. We will reconvene in a few minutes to discuss with you our decision." Mr. Crater chimed in, "If you can't satisfy your case, you will be fired on the spot. If I were you, I'd enjoy retirement. These people don't care about you. The government has paid them as if you were still a full-time employer. They didn't even care about the workers killing themselves with overtime. Let Anthony take care of you. He's a good guy." I snapped back, "Oh no he isn't and how dare you to tell me to take this laying down without defending myself. My marriage is in grave danger and I want and need to keep my career. Your services are no longer needed. Keep quiet, which is what you've been good at during this meeting. They returned within minutes, "We're sorry! You have until 3 p. m., today to prove justification as to why you voluntarily abandoned your job. If not, we will need a resignation letter at that time." I took a deep breath, "Do what's necessary for you. I will not be quitting my job because I have provided all necessary documents to prove my case; however, HR is known for not placing important documents or adding in documents to workers files; therefore, I will be contacting them immediately to personally check my records." Just say I reported Mr. Crater's remarks and he was immediately fired because the hearing was recorded. I was sure to keep all of my original copies and although they had copies as well, the dates never changed as to when I submitted the first physician's letter to return to work in December. I had done everything required of me and the only person to clear me was Ms. Lori who died the next day. As I stated to the panel, the sign in/out sheet revealed I was there at 7 a.m. I stopped by the hair salon and had most of my hair chopped off since it had been shedding due to stress, the surgeries, and strong narcotics. As for Anthony, he hadn't made much effort of upholding our contract. After reviewing our monthly spreadsheet, I realized we were in the red again since Mr. Big Spender had to impress his family with our unnecessary expensive July party. We were never able to recover and catch up after that. I cried all the way home and when I arrived, he didn't even notice my puffy, red eyes. It hurt that he never asked me about the meeting. I stood in front of him and all he said was, "Why are you standing there?" I shook my head, "You don't see it?" He frowned, "Huh? What are you talking about? I don't see what you want me to see girlfriend!" I turned back to look at him before I walked away, "ME." I turned back, "We're going to lose this house because too much money was spent for the party, the storage, and extension of the porch. It placed us in deep debt. You should've saved all of your bonus checks and got a part-time job as you originally said you would. You don't seem to see the debt we're in." He ignored my comment about the debt, "What do you want for Valentine's Day and your birthday?" I was disgusted, "Are you serious right now? I want absolutely nothing! We've gotta talk about a plan of survival not flowers and cake. I'm focused on needs not wants." He scoffed and walked away. I was too exhausted to cook, so I ordered pizza for Anthony to take to work. Before I laid down for a nap, I left him a note that read, *I ordered pizza for your lunch, Signed, Kay.* Shortly thereafter, Shannon came in and tapped me on my foot waking me up from a tormenting nightmare about a witch with long claws getting closer to her, "Momma, I'm home and dad said thanks for the pizza, but don't make it a habit, whatever that meant." She stared at my face, "Why are you sweating and breathing hard? Did you have a nightmare?"

February 14th Hate Day; Not Love Day

Anthony's mom had become ill and his money was a little short. Knowing this, I had previously opened up a second account with $200 in it for emergency purposes only because of Anthony's poor financial decisions. Apparently, he had forgotten all about that account. I felt bad that he didn't have money to get to his mom, so, I withdrew it all and closed the account. I handed him the money, "Here' $200, go take care of your mother." He looked at me with this wicked grin on his face as if to say, *she fell for it again!* Frankly, I didn't care what he did with the money, I just wanted to make sure that I did the right thing in God's sight. We had an understanding that both of our moms were sick and we were going to do everything we could to take care of them. A few days later, Anthony finally returned home from Ga from visiting his mother who was in ICU. I returned home at about 2:30 that afternoon after taking my mom to her counseling session and running a few errands of my own. To my surprise sitting on the table was an expensive bottle of perfume, a beautiful large crystal vase of roses, with a lovely pink bow wrapped around it, and a card signed, *For my wife, Ant.* Although it was a kind gesture, Anthony knew how I felt about gifts especially since multiple bills were past due causing our finances to be in red (Extremely Late) including our mortgage. The amount he spent on those gifts could've had our cable turned back on or could've have went towards our mortgage. To me, it seemed like his priorities weren't in order. I decided to heat up some fried chicken from the day before. So, I whipped up some cream potatoes and gravy, boiled corn on the cob with butter, a tossed salad, dinner rolls with homemade lemonade. Anthony walked in and looked at me as I cooked, "Man, I'm tired, but I'm gonna head to work and get some sleep during my break. Hopefully I won't get caught. Lord knows I'm the only one bringing in real money." The Lord quickened my spirit, "Be Still daughter and know that I am God." So, I bridled my tongue and shut my mouth. After cooking, I sat down at the computer and started another spread sheet. I knew there wouldn't be time to discuss it because he was in a rush (Per Usual) but I knew He couldn't help but to see all of the numbers circled in red, representing our total debt amount, late fees, final notices, and debt collectors. He looked at me, "Where's my lunch?" I turned to him calmly, "It's packed in your lunch container, the salad and Vinaigrette dressing is separate. Oh, and I would rather get our finances straight than to receive gifts. That to me is more important, but thank you for the kind gesture." He scoffed, "I get it Kay. I'm done talking about it though." (Translation: We've Had This Conversation Before) I shook my head, "I'll be up when you get off, then we can discuss it. Before he left, he inspected his lunch, "Go figure!" With an eyebrow raised and my lips pursed together, I waited for the rest of his complaint. He scoffed, "Fried chicken" again?" I shot back as I continued to review our bills, "We're not above leftovers Ant. We had leftover spaghetti last week. You know I don't cook every day. Especially since I have to care for mama and my therapy plays a huge factor." He raised his voice, "For your information, you served me fried chicken last week and it was bloody in the middle." As I shook my head, I looked up at him, "I'm sorry, me and Shannon's chicken were just fine. I offered you baked or broiled dishes, but you insisted on fried chicken at the last minute. I'll do better not to be in a rush next time. Besides, I don't claim to be a gourmet chef." Sarcastically he replied, "You need to learn your place WOMAN and take care of your home first. You and your mama need to take a back seat like they did back in the day." To me, it were as if he hated his own race because his conversation about the African American race always was so negative. I could feel the heat rise in my throat, but instead, I spoke within, "Peace be still!!! I'm sorry you feel this way. You can take it or not." I extended my hand, "Here, you can have my last $20.00 for gas and buy you some lunch on your way to work." His nose wrinkles, "You can't be serious. You know I can't be late. I guess you want me to be out of a job like you." I was fed up with his sarcasm and constant shots at me about my job, so, I shot back, "Seriously Ant. I'm receiving Social Security and Pension because of my disability and my invested time. If it were not from God's grace and mercy, I wouldn't be receiving those blessings and not to mention, I qualified for it. The sad part is you know that, but you continue to throw it in my face." He smirked, "You over here taking cooking classes, but what you really need is some remedial math classes since you got so much time on your hand to calculate things. Do the math, that aint no blessing, that's a curse. Know the difference. Compared to your income before quitting, you caused this household to lose $2000.00 a month that would cause us not to be in debt." I took a step back, "Back up! You're in my space. I can feel and smell your breath and that means you're too close. Aren't you running late for work? It's sad that you're trying to pick a fight with me. It's just chicken." Reality is, the fight wasn't about the chicken. It was deeper than that. We had been tip toeing around the pink elephant since the discovery of the camera amongst many other things. You could literally see the devil in this man's eyes and it was making me angrier by the second as to how he was allowing this controlling spirit to bully him into bullying me. I sat down at the table to eat my salad with vinaigrette dressing and hot soup with a dash of tabasco sauce in it, and a glass of ice-cold lemonade. He laughed, "If this were a real fight, I'd be whooping your lazy behind." Still seated, I looked up at him, "If it's gonna make you feel like a man, then do what you must." He walked over to the table, "You should never provoke me!" To my surprise, he reached down and splashed my salad and that hot bowl of soup in my face; mind you with tabasco sauce in it. He then grabbed by my glass of lemonade, poured it on my head, and broke the glass on the floor. I tried to knock him over as I struggled to the sink screaming, "My eyes, my eyes. I need to wash my eyes." He tried to break his fall by holding onto the counter and knocked over his lunch. I was furious, "You need to leave right now or I'm calling the police. This is not how Christ loved the church or how scripture tells a man to treat his wife. Your behavior is disgraceful and I'm so over it at this point." He nonchalantly left without a word. I'm so grateful to God that Shannon had to stay after school to decorate for a sweetheart daddy and daughter dance. Lord knows she had already experienced enough toxic trauma and witnessing what this man had just done to me would have caused even the more stress for her. I reached for my phone and texted another parent, *hey...please drop Shannon off for me*. I fell to my knees, "Lord, do I fight or flight this battle?" Before I could finish praying, Shannon had made it home, "Momma, let me show you the pictures I took—" She reached down looking at my clothes and began touching my wet hair,

"OMG! What in the world happened?" Salad and soup were all over me and everywhere else and so was the lunch I had prepared for Anthony. She looked around, "Where is he?" I reached for her hand, "I'm okay." Through heavy breathing, she shook her head, "I hate him. You deserve better than this momma and so do I." And she was right! As I got up from the floor, I looked at her, "Baby just help me clean up this mess. I promise, this won't happen again." Fifteen minutes later I heard Shannon scream, "Momma, he's back." I put on my robe and grabbed a bat from behind the door, "Look at me honey, you're gonna make matters worse." We walked towards the door, not knowing what was about to happen. Shannon grabbed a knife and stood behind me with her hand behind her back. I thought to myself, *Kay, we don't fight against flesh and blood.* Then, I began to pray, "Lord please protect us and calm his spirit." He quietly opened the door, rushed by us as if there were an urgency, and grabbed something from the top of the cabinet, placed it inside his pocket without one word, and rushed back out. I looked back at Shannon, "Did you see what he grabbed?" She shook her head, "No ma'am it must've been small because he put it inside of his pocket. There weren't any wires." She mumbled to herself with a frown on her face. My brows met, "What is it baby-girl?" She stood by as if deja vou visited her, "It was probably another camera." My mouth became dry as my heart began to race. Curiosity set in, "What makes you say that?" She walked closer to me, "Because the camera you found wasn't the only one." I felt faint, "Let's sit down over a glass of lemonade and talk about it. Is that ok?" She placed her finger over her lips and pointed outside to our newly built extended porch. I shook my head ok. I took a breath to calm my shaking hands and began praying Psalms 23 and Isaiah 45:2, "The Lord is my shepherd I shall not want ... I will fear no evil, for thou art with me. Dear Jesus please make this crooked place straight. Lord whatever my baby has to tell me good, bad, or ugly please prepare me and give me the strength to stand still dear Jesus." We sat in the swing and sipped on our lemonade. "Shannon, before you speak, just know that I love you, Jesus loves you, and I trust you. I'm gonna do everything I can to protect you." She lowered her head, "How mama? You took him back after you found the first camera. You stayed with him even after he proposed to you the second time." My heart was broken, "Baby, I believe in second chances. I believe in giving people the benefit of the doubt." I refreshed her memory, "Remember how you lied about what you were doing in the bathroom, right. I gave you a second chance when you told me and the therapist the truth. It's the same with God. He gave me so many undeserving chances after letting Him down too even when I repented for my wrongs. His grace and mercy kept me baby." She seemed confident that she could now open up to me, "But momma what if you give a person a chance to change and they don't but they just get worse?" Taken back, I asked, "Like your dad?" She nodded, "Yes." I lifted her chin, "No more worries. We're leaving and I'm divorcing him." She began to cry, "God forgive me, but I don't want him in my life anymore." I squeezed her hand, "Go on baby, you can tell me anything. I can't help you, if I don't know how." She looked away and began to stutter, "So, so, so." I reached for her hand, "Take your time." A tear fell down her face, "Mr. Rappt put three more cameras in my bathroom!" I panicked, "I can't breathe...where?" She wiped away her tears, "I was tying my shoe laces while sitting on the toilet and I saw one like the one you found behind the towel under the sink counter. Another one in the air condition vent above my toilet, and the third inside my wicker basket, hidden under my wash clothes with a hole cut in it." I was pissed, "Is that why we're out here? Do you believe the house is bugged?" She nodded once more, "Yes ma'am. I think that's what he got out of the bedroom just now." She reached for her phone, "He even texted me and told me to return the first one. He said, 'I know what you got good girl. You better put it on my desk like a good girl or else...' Then he said, 'Show me that you deleted the message when I see you." She continued, "Momma, I even grabbed a broom and knocked a camera down from the vent and threw it away, just as I did the one in the basket. I could feel anger knocking at my door, "Where are the cameras now?" At that point, I opened the door to anger and his crew, but I had to remain calm for my baby to get it all out. "Honey you could have forwarded it to me or anyone else." As I continued taking pictures, she pointed, "That's where the cameras were. That's why he would beat me so bad when you were gone. I was scared then and I still am now. The only reason why I'm telling you now is because you said you're leaving him. You haven't changed your mind, have you? Momma, you're divorcing him," she paused, "Right mama? He's so mean to me and you. No matter what you do to keep this family happy, he gets worse. He's so hateful. He's gonna get me for telling you!" I looked at her with reassuring eyes, "Oh no he won't. Not over my dead body." I grabbed her hand, "Shannon none of this is your fault. You can tell me the truth. I promise, I believe you honey!" Avoiding eye contact, the feeling of shame lowered her gaze not because she was lying but because she was embarrassed. She took a deep breath, "You remember when me and da— Mr. Rappt were playing WWE and we were wrestling?" I nodded, "Yeah go on." She looked over at me, "He didn't graze my boobs as he had you to be believe." As she continued, I could feel a fight within and it wasn't a Holy one. "Momma, he grabbed my breast and squeezed both of

159

them really hard and it hurt. I jumped up and ran to my room and locked the door. He ran behind me and said, 'Hey I'm sorry, it was just a rough game. Don't tell your mom. You know she over reacts about everything and would want to take you to the doctor. A few hours later I got a pink purse and shoes. (This Here Is a Pedophiles Best Trick. It's Called Grooming) I calmed myself, "He told me his brother gave you that as a belated birthday gift." Shannon shook her head, "He lied. He went on base, charged it, and stuffed the receipt in his pocket." I turned her face towards me, "Look at me! This is not your FAULT. I just wish you had told me sooner." She shook her head, "Momma, I'm sorry. I found all of them at different times when you were in the hospital and taking care of granny. I don't know why I would always find them in the mornings." I was beyond livid. This pedophile must have put them in her room at night. There's no telling what else he could've been trying to do. Was this pedophile watching her as she slept? What the hell? Yet again, this demon has violated my baby privacy, stripped her of her innocence, groomed her as a pedophile does, committed a crime and had the audacity to threaten her through text. He basically violated the contract he signed and agreed to, then spit on our vows in every way and that was it for me. I hugged Shannon, "I'm gonna make this right with God's help and He's gonna make what the devil meant for bad work for our good." She hugged me and let out a sound of relief, "It felt so good to tell you. I love you mama." As we walked back inside and saw the vase of roses, I cried, and threw them on the center of our floor that read, Team Rappt. At the sound of my screaming, my neighbors' dogs began to bark. Shannon placed her hand over her ears, "Mama, what you do that for?" I couldn't shake it, "How could I not know. I'm sorry Shannon. I had to let it out." Before I knew it, my nose was bleeding. Shannon ran to bathroom and came back with some tissue. By then, my blood pressure was so high that I felt faint. I reached for my phone, "Has Anthony hurt you anywhere else?" She knew exactly what I was asking her, "Momma, I'm a virgin. He didn't rape me with his penis, but his hands did!" Feeling nauseated, I covered my mouth in disbelief, "Yes he did and he's going to reap what he sowed too." There was a hard bang on the door. It was my Ride or Die chic Candy. She walked in and saw the house in a mess, but at this point, I didn't care. She grabbed me and hugged me as her daughter ran by, "Hi Aunty Kate. Where's Shan?" I pointed towards her room. Tears flooded my face as my knees buckled. Candy stepped over the splattered food in the kitchen, swooped me up, laid me on the couch, and gave me water and a paper towel for my bleeding nose. She sat down next to me, "You were heavy on my heart and the Lord had me to turn around to see about you." She paused, "What's

161

happening?" I could hear her daughter Mandy say, "Uh oh, no Shan." They were like sisters and I knew Shannon had told her some of our horror. Besides, she needed someone she could vent to as well. I just wished she would have told her sooner. I began to tell Candy what happened. Before I knew it, she stood up with tears in her eyes, "This is the last time that pervert gone make you cry or touch my niece ever again. He needs his head stomped in." She gathered herself, "You're a great wife and he don't even appreciate the blessing God gave him. Uhhhh, he's so stupid." She took a deep breath before continuing, "Well, the Lord giveth and He also taketh away. Go get your stuff and let's get the heck outta this hellhole." I reached for Candy's hand, "Please stop yelling, that ain't gonna help." She scoffed, "At least I aint cussing like a sailor. I'll go to the alter Sunday and repent, but right now, I'm madder than a mosquito in a mannequin factory." Confused, I looked at her, "Wait! What the what? Shut your dry humor mouth chile." She giggled, "I yell and curse when I vent and from the looks of it, that broken vase made you feel good too. You see sis we both vent differently." I smiled, "I'm not judging you girlfriend. It's just that I've let my child down in so many ways already. I didn't want her to hear me talking negative. I've been cussing, just not in her presence. I thought I was delivered from the potty mouth too, but I guess not." Candy scoffed, "What you need

162

deliverance from is blaming yourself for this crap. Let's get outta here now because ya'll ain't safe here. We'll pray for the best steps for you and Shannon once we leave." She went to Shannon's room to check on her and when she returned to my room ten minutes later, she found me with my gun behind my back. I looked at her, "Take Shannon to Marie's house and I'll get there later after I clean up the kitchen." She shook her head, "Girl please game recognize game. Killing that man with that loaded gun will send you straight to prison and him to hell. That's premeditated murder; not self-defense and Shannon needs you. Honey, you better remember that we don't fight against flesh and blood. God said vengeance is His and He shall repay. In other words, He don't need your help." She reached for my hand, "I know you're hurting and I can't even begin to imagine your rage. You cra cra like me! We'll go to the grave and jail for ours, but not to hell ok. That prick ain't worth it." I came back to my senses, removed the clip, discharged the single bullet in the chamber, and gave it to her. After gathering my thoughts, I packed just a few things unlike the first time I left. It was just stuff. I knew right then that I no longer wanted Mr. Anthony Rappt as my husband. I cried at the thought of having to figure out how to raise teenager on a fixed income all by myself, but there was a joy in knowing that God would always provide. Besides, our peace of mind was more valuable than it all. Candy called my mom and sister and explained to them what happened. I was too exhausted mentally and emotionally to tell what transpired again. Before she ended the call, she smiled, "We're definitely on our way this time." I could hear my mom say, "Come on before we come over there packing ready to unload!" Candy laughed, "Ya'll Simpson's ain't nothing to play with."

Confronting A Demon

I texted Anthony, *I'm down the street. I need to tell you something.* He replied, *yeah, I've got a lot to say as well, but ladies first.* Mama always told me to never let anyone see me sweat. So, I stepped of out the car looking like fine wine and an undamaged queen. I walked in and stood next to the table where he had gifts, tulips, and champagne with carefully selected wedding music playing in the background. He stood up and pulled out the chair, "Wow! You look stunning. Here, have a sip before we start talking." Champagne bubbles not fizz. I immediately declined his offer. I stood with my hand in my pocket ready to unload if necessary, "This won't take long. I just filed for a divorce and a restraining order with the police department." I placed the documents on the table, "Here's your copy. My unlimited resources will be here to move out our things in the morning.

There's no need for you to be here. It'll only be a distraction." I continued with complete confidence, "I'm not gonna to beat a around the bush. I don't love or like you anymore. You brought out the worse in me. All you did for me was constantly make me cry. I tried to be a good wife, but you punished me for medically retiring and you've hurt my daughter for the last time." He slammed his hands on the table and yelled, "No! You can't divorce me first. If you didn't cooperate on my terms, accept all of these expensive gifts, and go with me to therapy to work out this mess that's mostly your fault, I was gonna divorce you anyway. But hey, we can make this work, especially since you've gotten your job back." He paused, "Right?" As I stood up to leave, he scoffed, "Oh, so you think you cute? Go ahead and leave, I already got me somebody that looks even better waiting for this to be over." He smirked, "Besides, no one is gonna want you with that disease and that lazy little g—" Before I knew it, I had my pistol pointed at his chest, "Don't you ever speak of my daughter again. Stay away from me and mine. The police are outside and my brother is nearby. We're done. I'll see you in court." He smirked, "So you think you're Primadonna?" I took a deep breath, "No, I'm a child of The Most High King and all I care about in the end is to be called His Servant." I moved the gun away from his chest and coughed up a laugh, "You're not even worth this bullet.

Vengeance is mine said the Lord and He shall repay you for all you've done to me and my baby. You shall reap what you sow." As I walked away, I looked back, "But don't tempt me, I'm not totally delivered." He carefully sat down as I walked out and slammed the door.

Suck It Up and Move Forward

Annoyed and over everything pertaining to this marriage, I decided to pawn my wedding ring and take out a for $5,000 loan, rent a U-Haul, and call as many people as I could to help me move all in one day and prayed for a smooth and quick transition. We worked nonstop for ten grueling hours with only an hour to eat lunch. I had previously gotten everything necessary for the move down to the hand trucks being sure to leave nothing behind. Each person had a designated room to pack for a smooth and quick transition. As we continued to pack, I had three tech savvy people attempting to download data from his hard drive although we knew there was a possibility that everything was destroyed. As I stood by watching, I scratched my head, "This hard drive looks totally different. I think he's replaced it." All of a sudden, Anthony showed up unexpectedly putting everyone on edge. You could see the frustration in his eyes when he saw my cousin unplugging and packing up all of my office furniture and computer. In the midst of us being in the office, Anthony decided to start making multiple copies of his church programs (Strange) I looked at my cousin, "Keep an eye on him." But reality was, he was keeping an eye on us. Anthony then walked into the master bathroom and startled my sister Leslie when he attempted to hug her. As she pushed him off of her, I screamed, "Anthony, you need to leave." As he walked out, they didn't say a word to each other. I called the police to assist us if he returned. Due to him being part owner of the home, they couldn't arrest him because he hadn't harmed or threatened anyone. Thank God that Shannon was at church for a Black History program because it saved her from having to witness all of this. As I began packing Shannon's room, it was apparent that her organizational skills were absent, so I asked everyone to leave to deal with it alone and spare her some dignity. As I began moving things around, things that were hidden were now in plain sight, an apparent cry for help. I sat down on her bed in tears, "God, why my baby? Why did she have to have ADHD and this God awful pedophile to violate her?" I took a deep breath, "By Jesus stripes, she is healed," but the tears wouldn't stop falling and before I knew it, Anthony came back once more, "You cleaning out huh? Can I at least keep the recliner? It's my Father's Day gift." I was livid, "You can take that recliner, this shell of a house, and your empty soul, and shove it all where the sun don't shine. Just let me leave in peace. Why are you even back here again?" Everyone stopped what they were doing and came to where we were ready for him to make the wrong move. My cousin cleared his throat, "Kay, the police wants to see you." Anthony lifted his hands as if in surrender, "I don't want no trouble man." My brother stood by with his fist balled, "Jesus Keep Me Near the Cross." The police officers stood near as Anthony walked towards me, "Here's your extra car key and for what it's worth Happy Birthday!" I was so angry that I forgot it was my 49th birthday. I took a deep breath and left. I was emotionally drained. I figured I could get my office chair and the other things later. When we finally left, I was escorted all the way to my sister Marie and my mom's house for safety precautions. When we finally arrived, I sat in that truck and sobbed for a full 10 minutes. God said release, so I did. I got out of the U-Haul truck and walked in to everyone screaming, "HAPPY BIRTHDAY KAY!" Even with everyone exhausted from helping me move, they took out the time to surprise me with cake, balloons, cards, flowers and several gift bags. A tear flowed down my face as momma looked at me, "Why are you crying?" I wiped the tears from my eyes, "Because I can breathe and we're finally safe." Marie placed her hand on my back, "Suck it up Kay and move forward." Although what she said was true, it just wasn't the right time to say it. How could she not understand? I had lost my job, my house, and my spouse within the same week. Momma intervened, "Kay, sit down, eat, and relax, you're home now." I thanked everyone and embraced each person, and made a wish that went a little like this, *I wish that I would one day have the courage to tell our story and wonder how we made it over and perhaps encourage someone else to have a voice to seek help and change.* I then smiled and blew out the candles. That night, Shannon decided to sleep in the room with me. We later prayed and fell asleep. The following Monday I hired Attorney Ova; the best attorney money could buy in the South and paid my retainer. She was a beast. Her motto was *When you want your marriage to be over, see Attorney Ova for your Transitioning.* Shortly thereafter, local authorities placed me with the DA that took our case, a restraining order was finally in place, and DHR had been informed of the situation, as well as Shannon's school counselor. Shannon then had a physical exam to determine if she was a virgin. Praise God she was. During this full-blown investigation she began the gruesome 30 sessions of therapy that were ordered by DHR in which was very hard for her. I looked at her, "Baby, I know it's hard, but you have to go through the necessary process." I wiped the tear from her eyes, "I'm here with you every step of the way. All you have to do is tell the truth." She was later diagnosed with PTSD and prescribed the same meds as my mom and I was prescribed meds for insomnia. Not to mention that our privacy clearly wasn't respected because our former neighbors consistently inquired of our sudden move. There was a man named Pastor Travis, his wife Rachel, and their five daughters who lived directly across the street. I used to always want to have bible study with them, but Anthony was against the mixed nuts faith meetings as he called it. When I finally had the opportunity to talk with them, I poured them a big bowl of honest heart, "My husband allegedly cheated on me and molested my daughter. Now, I'm divorcing him. The accusations as the DA called it are being investigated." I looked at the wife and back to Pastor Travis, "I attempted to resign from my secretary position and told my pastor and first lady what happened, but they wouldn't allow me to leave any part of the ministry. They told me that if I didn't want to be with him or if I didn't love him, I was in order to leave and protect my daughter Shannon. They simply wanted me to keep my mind focused on kingdom building." Even in all of this, I had to take care of my mother full time. Being that there was no down time to process or properly grieve, I cried every night for months. You would have thought that my troubles were officially over, but rebellion began to take over Shannon and I became her target. She looked at me, "You should've known something was wrong."

I had no reply. Her grades and weight began to significantly decline, I caught her watching porn three different times on her phone, and I began seeing scars and fresh bruises on her hands and forearm. Since I didn't know what was going on, I made her move into my room with me. She was livid and everything else began to spill over. "Mom, you don't get it. I have a daddy that doesn't want me and the one you married treated me like a sex object and tried to rape me." She took a deep breath, "I felt like I needed to punish myself for not telling you. That's why you see the scars and bruises." I lowered and shook my head, "This is the trick of the enemy and if this doesn't stop, you'll go from pinching to cutting, then burning. You can't satisfy abnormal sensation. So, stop self-mutilating yourself as a coping mechanism!" I gently grabbed her arm, "Shannon, none of this is your fault. I can understand that this situation has bruised you, but you're not broken and this tragedy will only make you wiser than before." I leaned over to hug her, "I love you and I'm sorry I didn't pay attention when people warned me that you were in danger. Baby, I heard you in your bravery when I realized that you were Sandra in the park. I was brave enough to leave him and brave enough to get all appropriate authorities involved to ensure your safety. I'm sorry this happened to you. I don't think you understand, I'll go to jail or to the grave for you." She smiled and then we cried and hugged it out. But something was still wrong. Therapy, medications, nor myself could seem to get through to Shannon. So, one day my nephew Lovell sat down and had a talk with her. "Listen Shannon, this thing that you're doing is not gonna take the pain away. You've gotta promise me that you will never hurt yourself again. If you're feeling bad, all you have to do is call me." Just say, Lovell got through to her and she started using coco butter and a prescribed cream for the scars and infections. I was relieved, grateful, and appreciative that we had a great support system, but I hated being single because I had to adjust to sleeping alone, being a single parent with limited income, sleepless nights, and living with my family amongst other things. But God made things better and as time passed, I stopped living in fear and no longer carried an authorized loaded weapon. Just say, I slept at night and the gossiping seemed to cease. But I felt horrible about saying something to a sister at the church about putting me on the singles outing list. Just say I had to apologize to her later, then I kindly informed her that I no longer wanted to be associated with the single life. Three months after our separation, I sat in the audience and listened as Shannon stood on the stage during a Miss Mahogany pageant, "Your voice is everything so use it wisely. Tell someone that you trust if you're body or personal space is being violated. Tell someone if you're being touched inappropriately or if you're being molested. Remember, it's your voice. Never allow anyone to manipulate you into remaining silent." She then boldly looked at each judge, the audience filled with hundreds of people, and her fellow contestants with a raised voice in the mic, "I'm still strong, I'm standing, and I'm a survivor Thank you!" She received a standing ovation. I stood and applauded her bravery as tears of joy streamed down my face, "Whoop whoop, great job baby!" But down deep inside, I was saddened that my family couldn't make it to see my little queen come in as second runner up. After the pageant, a young man that we knew walked up to me, "Ms. Kay, is it okay if I give Shannon these red roses as a congratulatory gesture?" I smiled, "Absolutely." It was okay because I had received counseling from his parents before, besides, we were all good friends. He smiled, "Shannon was the prettiest contestant up there. She didn't look made up." I smiled once more, "I concur, but I'm bias." Shannon loved him and his family, so after she turned sixteen and was in a good emotional space, I gave them permission to date. As time went on, I began to heal emotionally from a marriage designed to break me. Six months I was divorced! He fought me during mediation to pay alimony and our income tax return, instead I willfully gave up the house and was awarded my last name. One day, I stopped by the house to pick up the last of my furniture and when I arrived, there was a letter on the porch for Shannon that read, *Things could have been better on both of our parts. The breakdown of our marriage was not your fault. Shannon, if you ever need me, just call.* Needless to say, I took the letter to the DA's office immediately. When we went before the grand jury, they questioned him about it because there was an active restraining order against him. When called to come forth, the lies rolled off his tongue like water, "Marie knew about me purchasing the camera and so did Shannon's mother." He looked at the jury, "She gave me consent." Another bald faced lie that only he could tell. Just say he walked with no charges against him because of my inexperienced, incompetent detective who forgot to submit the DHR investigation, and the questioning of Shannon and I as well as my sister. A year later, Shannon continued therapy, stopped hurting herself, stopped blaming me, and her grades and attitude improved; however, that all later changed. In January, Shannon went from progressing to digressing and had to be put her back on anxiety meds. Due to her digressing, the therapist sent a detailed letter to the DA's office informing them that she was ready to testify, but not in in the same room as Anthony. To make sure that she didn't miss her opportunity to testify, we requested for accommodations to be made. Sadly, that didn't happen. Being that Shannon never had to take the stand, the DA's office would later inform us of the juror's decision, so we went on with our lives. A few days later, I got dressed thinking I was going to Red Lobster with my family for my 50th birthday. I was elated to find out they were surprising me with an all purple party. Thank God my dress was purple. Marie spearheaded the entire event and got the venue, food, decorations, D.J., and invites just for me with the help of Leslie and Edward. I received many gifts and well wishes as everyone expressed their love one way or another. The celebration was a blast and I felt special and blessed. March came and still no mail or call in regards to the case, so I went to the DA's office and inquired of their decision. Once again, the detectives dropped the ball. They looked me straight in the eyes, "We're sorry. Due to circumstantial evidence, Shannon's inability to testify in front of Mr. Rappt, and no recorded footage, the case was closed and there was no indictment." I fainted and found myself waking up in our local ER with an oxygen mask on my face. No one knew I was there except for the detective. I looked at him, "Please leave. My family will pick me up." I was later told by the DA that my case couldn't be appealed due to it being a Federal case and it would have to start over on civil bases. As I waited to be picked up, I prayed for the words to tell Shannon. After arriving home, I shared this God-awful news with her, she scoffed, "I can't go through this again mom. He's invisible to me. Just let God do the rest and fight this battle. You believed in me and fought for me and I couldn't have asked for better." I will never underestimate her resilience. She later graduated from therapy, threw her pills away, and made the honor roll by the time we moved out of my family's house into our own home. During our eleven o'clock service, the pastor preached a powerful message that went a little like this, *Our God has not given us a spirit of fear, but of power, love, and a sound mind. Forgive those that mistreat you and know that vengeance is God's and He shall repay.* Just say, after that message, the nightmares were over. Not long thereafter someone thought it was important to inform me that Anthony was now married to Bethany, yeah, his ex, but my prayer was that she didn't have a daughter for him to violate. Although Shannon and I had to start over from the ground up (Humble Beginnings), I wouldn't trade it for our safety, a peace of mind, and our now sweet sleep. Over time, as we shared our story with different mothers, daughters, and groups, we too learned that they were victims of sexual assault and or rape, mainly by men they knew. The number of incidents that had never been reported baffled me because they were left to live their lives in shame, embarrassment, and fear. Although Shannon and I were bruised, we were not broken. We took a stand in going before the legal system, taking the necessary steps for counseling, and speaking our truth. Although our truth was concealed under the microscope of disguise, it is now revealed by faith that ALL hidden things have been made known. Use your voice without fear and know that The Lord will fight your battles.

Favorite Scripture: Proverbs 3:18 "She is a tree of life to them that lay hold upon her: and happy is every one that retaineth her." (KJV)

Favorite Quotes: "Speak up for those who cannot speak for themselves." "I never knew how strong I was until I had to forgive someone who wasn't sorry and accept apologies I never received." **Maya Angelou,** "If someone shows you their real self, believe them the first time." **Former CEO, Hewlett-Packard by Carla Fiorina,** "A man does not get respect from other men if he is disrespectful to women. **Tony Morrison,** "If there is a book that you want to read that hasn't been written yet, you must be the 'ONE' to write it." **Jennifer Mahand-Smith,** "You're gonna bless so many people." **Corcelia Hornsby-Lampley,** "You weren't meant to fit in, but to stand out." **Casandra Ware,** "This too shall pass." **Crystal James,** "From beginning til the end, you listened, advised, and supported us." **Ken Valrie,** "Get off your a@@ and just write the book, who cares what they say or think." **Yalanda Brooks,** "Be patient!" **Robin McKinney and Yolanda Daniels-Milton,** "Real love exists!" **Shekaunna T. McCauley** "Mom stop crying... You can do this. We're still here!"

www.ingramcontent.com/pod-product-compliance
Lightning Source LLC
Chambersburg PA
CBHW021010180626
46814CB00003B/1231